Jacob nearly dropped his great sword. He staggered back, his eyes the size of moons. Kern and Miltiades froze open-mouthed, warhammers raised and arm muscles tight. Trandon shielded his eyes and crouched down, his quarterstaff rolling away on the floor.

Noph choked on his terror. He could not look away from the beautiful, inhuman face that almost touched the far side of the wall.

"We are here," said the voice in the room. "We are the emperor of Doegan."

FORGOTTEN REALMS
Fantasy Adventure ®

The DOUBLE DIAMOND TRIANGLE SAGA™

FORGOTTEN REALMS

Fantasy Adventure

The DOUBLE DIAMOND TRIANGLE SAGA™

Part 4

ERRAND OF MERCY

Roger E. Moore

ERRAND OF MERCY
©1998 TSR, Inc.
All Rights Reserved.

Distributed to the book trade in the United States by Random House, Inc. and in Canada by Random House of Canada Ltd. Distributed to the hobby, toy, and comic trade in the United States and Canada by regional distributors. Distributed worldwide by Wizards of the Coast, Inc. and regional distributors.

Cover art by Heather LeMay.

First Printing: February 1998
Printed in the United States of America.
Library of Congress Catalog Card Number: 96-90567

9 8 7 6 5 4 3 2 1

8637XXX1501

ISBN: 0-7869-0867-X

U.S., CANADA, ASIA,
PACIFIC, & LATIN AMERICA
Wizards of the Coast, Inc.
P.O. Box 707
Renton, WA 98057-0707
+1-206-624-0933

EUROPEAN HEADQUARTERS
Wizards of the Coast, Belgium
P.B. 34
2300 Turnhout
Belgium
+32-14-44-30-44

Visit our website at **www.tsr.com**

For John Michael Moore,
the best there is.

Prologue

"*Open in the name of the past and present lords of Waterdeep!*"

The warrior watched as the flowing veins of magic in the gate dimmed and faded in reaction to his words. A narrow ripple of yellow light rolled out swiftly from the center of the gate like a wavelet from a stone dropped into a pond. The center of the expanding circle was purest black. In a moment, the entire gate was darker than a bottomless pit, framed by two gigantic ivory tusks that glowed with a pale light.

The old warrior turned to look once at his fellows, four men and a woman who stared at the open gate in awe. He shrugged, then unslung his shield from his back and ran his left arm through the straps. Hefting his massive warhammer in his right hand, he studied the weapon silently, turned to the gate again, and stepped forward. He inhaled and instinctively held his breath, walking into the blackness in the center of the gate. Like that, he was gone.

His disappearance was so sudden that the youngest of the group, hardly more than a boy, gasped aloud. It seemed as if the gate had swallowed the warrior in silver armor alive. A few moments later, another warrior, a young man in armor made of golden scales, stepped forward. He held his own warhammer forward, ready to punch out at any foe or obstacle. Then he, too, was gone.

The four who were left glanced uneasily at each other. By unspoken agreement, the knight with the bright two-handed sword went next, followed by the gray-haired man in leathers, carrying his fighting staff out before him. When the older man had vanished, only the woman in robes and the youth remained. They talked quietly, then the young man pulled a knife from his boot, steeled himself, and went through the gate, too.

The woman watched him go. She sighed, then lifted her chin and spoke.

"Close in the name of the past and present lords of Waterdeep!"

A circular rainbow of light bloomed from the center of the blackness in the gate. In moments, the gate was as it had been only minutes before, veins of visible magic flowing across its surface. The woman swiftly left the area, descending the flight of stone steps that led away from the gate, sitting atop a small pyramid inside a huge, battle-stained room far underground.

At the only door leading out of the great chamber, the robed woman turned. Raising her arms, fingers spread, she took a deep breath and called out the words to the most powerful spell she knew. Her voice grew louder, and the ends of her long hair rose and separated, charging with electricity. At the crescendo of her spell, she shouted a single word and thrust her hands forward, pointing both her index fingers at the gate.

She forgot to blink. The lightning bolt was stamped on her retinas for an hour afterward, and she was half-deaf from the thunderclap as the crooked bolt, bright as the sun, sprang from her fingers to the gate—and blew it into a million pieces.

Chapter 1

A Serpent in the Kingdom's Bed

He began as nobody, one brown squalling infant among a hundred born that day among his conquered people, the Mar. He was sickly and his mother did not expect him to live long. It was months before his father finally named him Ikavi Garkim. He hoped the boy would make a good carpenter if he survived to his eighth year. His family was *tarok*, the lowest class of the Mar, and struggled

for food and money that the *bahrana*, the few
middle-class Mar, took for granted.

Ikavi survived many illnesses in his family's
one-room adobe home, lost in a sprawling slum
that spilled around the gray walls of Eldrinpar,
the seacoast capital of Doegan. His stubborn survival was not the only thing that made him different, though. His peculiarity became clear as soon
as he could speak. He acted before orders were
given him; he mouthed secret thoughts without
knowing their meaning.

At first everyone thought this was marvelous,
but in the end no one could tolerate it. No thought
was safe near him. Relatives and friends ceased to
visit the tiny home. Ikavi's parents punished him
for speaking their thoughts aloud; later, to gain
privacy, they simply sent him away, or else filled
their heads with mindless chants, songs, or
prayers when he was near. Ikavi frowned when
they did this, which unnerved them.

Other children found Ikavi's mind-reading annoying. They threw stones at him until he ran
back to his home or hid. Ikavi usually played by
himself in the hot, dusty streets of his neighborhood: a packed maze of low, baked-mud homes,
filled with the cries of children and the shouts of
adults. He stole food to survive, like every other
tarok child, but his style of theft grew from his
mind-reading abilities. As he became better at un-
derstanding the thoughts of those around him, he
simply picked up things—a piece of fruit, a silver
coin, a top, a folding knife—when no one was paying attention. He learned carpentry by reading his
father's thoughts, and he helped his sire carve

toys and idols or repair broken furniture on the dusty steps of their home.

Then on a hot summer afternoon a tanned, drunken soldier, one of the sharp-nosed conquerors called the Ffolk, staggered down Ikavi's home street after taking a wrong turn on the way back to his barracks. The poverty-stricken Mar fled before him, fearing the soldier would cut them down or otherwise abuse them. He could do this with impunity. No Mar had the rights of a Ffolk.

Ikavi's father was away at the market selling items they had carved the previous day. Ikavi himself sat on the steps of his home, a folding knife and a wooden figurine in his dirty hands. The soldier saw him, pointed, and shouted an order. Out of habit, Ikavi peered into the man's mind, intrigued by unfamiliar words and images. The man spoke and thought in the harsh consonants of the invaders' Thorass, not the liquid Maran tongue Ikavi knew.

Perhaps the soldier sensed this psychic intrusion and resented it, or perhaps Ikavi did not obey his orders quickly enough. The man drew his sword and lunged at the child. Ikavi's mother saw and rushed between them to block the blow. The angry soldier shoved the shrieking woman aside and turned to the disrespectful boy.

But the boy was already upon him, enraged that a soldier would lay hands on his mother. With the speed of a leopard, Ikavi stabbed the soldier in the heart before the drunken man could dodge the blow.

Ikavi, no one's fool, would have gotten away if

the dying soldier's comrades had not appeared just at that moment, looking for their inebriated companion. With little trouble, they chased and caught the Mar boy.

One soldier had an axe. In those days, it was the practice to immediately execute *tarok* troublemakers of any age without trial. The enraged soldiers forced Ikavi against the steps of his own home and bent down his head. His family looked on from a distance and screamed.

"Stop."

The word, spoken in Thorass, came out of thin air. Startled, the soldier lifting the axe drew back. The others looked up from their struggle to hold Ikavi down, searching the street for the speaker.

"Bring the boy alive to the palace, now," continued the voice. It was neither soft nor loud. It held neither emotion nor humanity. It reached into every hidden place up and down the street. The soldiers froze like frightened rabbits. They knew the voice well. The man with the axe dropped the weapon and hid his hands.

Wrestling the youth to his feet, three soldiers finally forced Ikavi to go with them, arms pinned behind his back. The last two soldiers picked up the axe and the body and sword of their comrade, then marched off to the palace behind the others.

Ikavi's hysterical family bewailed their loss. They knew Ikavi would die at the hands of the hated Ffolk. They mouthed empty words of revenge and fell asleep in their tears and sorrow.

Yet on the following morning there he was, right at the door of their home, not only alive but wearing the silk clothing of a Ffolk noble child. He

had with him a retinue of palace guards and a
nervous Ffolk healer who cured his mother's
bruises. Ikavi said little, only that the mage-king
himself had ordered that he stay at the palace
from now on. His family would not be punished.
His mother hugged him briefly, but let him go.
Everyone else in his family was too stunned to
react.

Ikavi went away. In the evenings he could be
seen standing in the high windows of the palace's
lone tower, looking down at the countless poor
dwellings beyond the city walls. He had been
saved by the mage-king of Doegan, Aetheric III,
the unseen master of Doegan's great bloodforge—
but saved for what? No one knew at first. The
haughty Ffolk of the palace hated the child's presence, especially as he'd slain a Ffolk soldier, but
they dared not challenge the mage-king's decree.

After his arrival at the palace, Ikavi was regu-
larly brought into the mage-king's meeting halls.
It soon became clear that he was being trained for
some purpose. The Ffolk soon feared little Ikavi
almost as much as they feared their mage-king,
for the boy's telepathic ability was combined with
a great knowledge of the kingdom and its people,
and many secrets beyond. Military officers and
priests were ordered to teach him all they knew.
Ikavi was given political and military powers,
which were gradually increased and sharpened.

In time, Ikavi Garkim was acknowledged to be
the mage-king's personal agent in Doegan. He was
loyal and patriotic, educated and well-spoken, determined and ruthless. At last the mage-king sent
his voice to the Chamber of Councilors and an-

nounced that Lord Ikavi Garkim was one of them. Doegan, said the mage-king, was infested with unseen forces that would bring it low unless they were stopped. Only Lord Garkim—a small, brown, flat-nosed outsider in a sea of white, sharp-nosed faces—could detect those unseen forces, and he had been given almost unlimited authority to root out such evil wherever he found it.

The other lords took to Ikavi as they would to a serpent in their beds, but they, too, knew a bit about the unseen forces arrayed against Doegan, and they felt their lives were better with the serpent at their sides than not. Left with no other choice, they smiled in his presence.

Ikavi Garkim had been nobody and was now the mage-king's right hand. But whether he was better off than before was a question not even Ikavi could answer.

* * * * *

Lord Ikavi Garkim, Councilor of Internal Investigations, returned to his old neighborhood an hour before dawn, twenty-six years after he had left. Twenty hand-picked soldiers were at his back and a hacking machete was in his right hand. No one noticed him or his soldiers as they walked down the deserted street in the half-light. They were invisible, covered by magic so that even a wizard would be hard pressed to find them, their boots wrapped in cloth to muffle their steps. The sky glowed pink in the east, the sun still low behind the distant mountains. The wind at their backs was cool, a breeze blowing from the shores of the Great Sea. A sparrow chirped from a rooftop.

Lord Garkim recognized the doorway where he had once sat and carved wooden toys at his father's side. He had steeled himself for this moment, but it still hurt. His fingers tightened on the thick leather grip of his machete.

Prepare yourselves, he ordered, sending his thoughts behind him to his soldiers. He sensed their excitement and fear. He took a breath, unaware that he was walking faster, then leaned forward into a dead run for the open doorway. *Now!* he signaled.

He went through the doorway with his left arm up, covering his face. The edge of the doorway suddenly blazed with red glyphs as he went through. Trap—

A roar of flame burned his skin from all sides. The pain, even muffled by his protective magic, was terrific. Instinctively he shut his eyes, saving them from being scorched along with his clothing and hair. He ran into someone and had the presence of mind to shove hard with his left hand, then hack down with his right. The razor-sharp machete slashed through flesh and bone. Stumbling over a carpet, Garkim and his screaming victim fell to the floor.

Garkim shoved himself up, keeping his eyes shut to boost his awareness of the thoughts around him. He could hardly have seen anything in the unlit house anyway. He hacked a second time at the struggling figure beneath him, then sensed more people around him and lashed out at the closest one. They were ragged figures who moments before had

been eating their morning meal. Garkim sensed
their alarm, read their sudden fears, knew their
plans to escape.

And smelled their meal. His nose was filled
with the stomach-churning odor. He nearly vom-
ited then, but redoubled his wild attacks and
fought down his nausea. Blows landed on his
arms, whether from fists or clubs he couldn't tell.
He got up to strike at a man trying to get behind
him. Someone else, a woman, grabbed one of his
legs and clumsily tried to force him down. The
air stank of fresh blood and burnt meat. Garkim
gripped his machete with both hands and fought
like a crazed man, the screams and curses of
those whom he wounded ringing through the
cramped room.

As Garkim killed the ragged people, he read
their minds. Accursed names and unspeakable
deeds blew by him in a typhoon wind. This one
had cut the throat of a girl who knew his secret.
That one, who spied on soldiers, was going to run
to a house across the street where he would hide
in a cellar. The woman biting into his left thigh
had sacrificed her baby to join this group. Garkim
knocked her away, then killed her with a blow to
the head.

No one was left standing near him. He opened
his eyes. The last ragged one alive was running
for the doorway, but suddenly stopped and ran
back toward him. The man must have seen what
had happened to the others who had fled into the
street. Garkim read his mind. It was the man
Garkim wanted most.

Garkim threw his machete hard at the man's

legs. The man cried out and stumbled when the blade hit. He crashed into a low table and fell, knocking several baskets down over him. Garkim was on him in an instant. His fingers caught the man's filthy hair and pulled his head back as far as it would go without breaking his neck.

"Your master!" Garkim shouted in Maran, one knee planted in the man's back. "Name your master!"

But there was no master in the man's thoughts. He had never seen his master, the high priest of the Fallen Temple. His dreams had told him what to do, only his dreams. The injured man's thoughts spilled out in a flood. Garkim read flickering images, listened to scattered words, and found nothing more of interest. For three decades he had studied the worst secrets imaginable and had seen horrors to fill ten lifetimes. The horrors present in this mind were no different.

Garkim picked up his machete and, with one movement, cut his prisoner's throat.

The victim's struggles quickly ceased. Garkim let go of the man's head and sat back on the floor, his right hand splashed with dripping warmth. All his energy had left him. His breath came in gasps. He tried to stand up, but nausea got to him and he fell, vomiting. His head was pounding. A sergeant helped him outside. Garkim was sick and sat, his head buried in his arms. He did not see the blanket-draped things from the one-room house that the rest of his soldiers dragged out into the street. The troops laid the blood-soaked bundles before the astonished eyes of the neighborhood *tarok*, who hung back from the stony-faced soldiers and what they brought into the morning light. Garkim merely sat in the street beside the wall of his childhood home, trembling as from a fever.

"My lord," said the sergeant later. "All is ready."

Garkim coughed, then slowly got to his feet. It was already dawn. His soldiers had finished cleaning out the house. A large pile of blanket-covered debris and a row of limp, ragged bodies occupied the center of the street.

Lord Garkim looked down at his uniform. He was as filthy and bloody as the bodies in the street. It did not matter. Nothing like that mattered to him most days now.

He nodded to the sergeant, who stepped back and faced the frightened crowd. "Citizens of the Imperial Reaches of Doegan!" the sergeant shouted in Maran. "Listen to the words of Lord Garkim!" He said "DOH kun" as some of the Mar did, instead of "DOH eh gen" with a hard g, as did the Ffolk. He then turned and nodded to Garkim, who was ready.

"These people you see dead before you were your neighbors!" Garkim cried in Maran, both arms raised the way Mar tribal elders did at clan meetings. "Look at them! Look at their faces! They lived among you, spoke with you, shared food with you! Now look at them! You ask yourself, why did we do this? Why did we kill them?"

He swiftly strode over to one of the blankets covering things pulled from the one-room house. He seized a corner and whipped the blanket back. He knew what lay beneath it. "See this! Look at what they ate this morning, as they prayed to the monsters that lead their Fallen Temple!"

Women and children looked down and shrieked; some fainted or ran. Grown men choked and drew back, swallowing. Hundreds of dark eyes rimmed with white stared down at the half-eaten meal that lay in the dust of the street. The soldiers glanced at it, then turned away with grim faces. They already knew who it had been.

Garkim flipped the blanket back down. Hundreds of wide eyes looked up at him. "You know me!" he shouted, his voice carrying easily over the crowd. "You remember that I was a boy here! I am one of you! I tell you that this"—his hand swept down to the blanket and the thing it covered on the street—"this is the work of evil, the work of monsters, not the work of *my* people! It is not *your* work! You must fight with me against the wickedness of the Fallen Temple! We must throw it down! If you go this way, you will lose your soul! You will not be Mar, nor even human! Be on guard against this evil, and help me destroy it!"

He felt exhaustion settle over him with chains of iron. His headache, ever present in the depths of his consciousness, grew in intensity. He wiped his face with his arm and noticed that his skin stung as if he were sunburned. He'd forgotten already about the fire runes. He waved to the sergeant, who pulled a small bottle from a pouch on his belt, unsealed the stopper, and walked down the row of ragged dead, emptying the contents of the bottle on them. Smoke billowed out where the liquid touched the bodies. Moments later, the dead burst into flames that consumed rags, hair, blood, and flesh alike. The soldiers and *tarok* stepped back from the pyre as oily black smoke rose over the street and into the dawn's bright light, carrying its stench across the awakening city and all within it.

Lord Garkim turned to leave. He stepped on a bit of debris brought out by his soldiers from the den of death. He looked down, then bent to pick it up.

It was the head of a broken hammer.

Garkim nodded and took it with him.

* * * * *

Lord Garkim was bathed and dressed in time to attend the regular midmorning councilors' meeting at the ministry building, adjacent to the palace. Word of his morning activities had preceded him. The other councilors were eager for any news he bore.

"You say that you and your men entered the house—" said the gray-bearded Lord Erling, Thorass as precise as ever.

"I went in alone," Lord Garkim corrected. "My men stayed outside to catch those who fled and to locate other escape routes, of which there were two. They later apprehended a man living across the street, another cultist who hid fugitives in his cellar."

"Did you use that improved form of invisibility on yourself and your men during your approach, the spell I recommended?" Lady Hetharn leaned forward, eyes bright with interest. A rivulet of sweat trickled from the corner of her brightly painted lips and coursed down over the first of her chins.

"Let Lord Garkim finish his story," said the

Council General with a sigh. "We can save technical questions for a bit."

Lord Garkim cleared his throat. "As I entered, I accidentally triggered the trap-runes on the doorframe, which admitted only other cultists. None of the group were wizards, so they somehow have access to such magic. The protective devices I had on loan from the armory shielded me from the flames, for the most part. Thereafter I was able to drive out some of the cultists and disable the others. The bodies were burned to prevent reanimation. We used a bottle of *liko agnar*, the liquid fire that Lady Hetharn's laboratory kindly provided for our department." He nodded to the lady, who smiled back with unconcealed pride.

"Disable?" Lord Erling said, confused. "You disabled them? I had thought you said you . . . well, that you—"

"I killed them, yes," said Lord Garkim readily. "However, because these cultists often animate their dead, it is as if killing them does not really *kill* them. I sometimes think I am merely disabling them until we can burn the bodies and truly destroy them. *Then*, and only then, are they dead and gone."

The short silence was broken by a subdued Lady Hetharn. "I am glad that your family was moved into different quarters last year, so that they were not there when . . . when those of the Fallen Temple—"

"Yes, and I share your relief, believe me," Garkim said with feeling. "I am sorry, however, that we could not save our Captain Taergen from the fate visited upon him after he was kidnapped.

My men and I will see to his proper burial tomorrow with full honors in the Field of Heroes. You are all, of course, invited to attend."

The other lords at the table nodded assent. Some swallowed and looked ill. Others stared in tight-lipped silence at the head of the broken hammer on the tabletop before Lord Garkim. All tried to imagine what sort of people would chop up a man and eat him for their morning meal.

Another sigh escaped from the Council General. "Let us move along," he said quickly. "We have eight dead cultists, one in custody, and no leaders or clues to their plots. Lady Hetharn advises me that we cannot connect any of them to the killing of the soldier and mail-rider outside Eldrinpar's walls the other day—yes, Lady Hetharn?"

"That was most likely the work of aerial monsters." Lady Hetharn spoke quickly and knowledgeably, back in her element. "There were no tracks beyond the immediate area, and the prints and claw marks we found suggest that giant eagles or griffons were the cause. They must have been attracted by the scent of the horses. We still need to perform certain divinations to—"

"Lord Garkim." The voice out of thin air killed all conversation on the spot.

"Yes, Your Majesty," said Lord Garkim, sitting back in his chair. He forced himself to relax, or at least to appear so.

"Go into the Vault of the Stone Arch, and prepare to greet those who arrive there. Bring them to the palace and ensure their comfort."

"Yes, Your Majesty," said Lord Garkim crisply. After a pause to make sure there were no other commands, he pushed back his chair and got to his feet. "My ladies and lords," he said to the others, bowing swiftly, then left the Chamber of Councilors, striding down the corridor for the stairs.

He shrugged as he went. The gods only knew who he was supposed to meet at the vault. The mage-king never explained himself, and it was useless to try to read his mind; his thoughts could not be read by anyone. No doubt this was a by-product of his long use of the bloodforge. Lord Garkim frowned as he descended the steps to the main hall of the ministry building. The people at the vault were doubtless just another "official complaints" delegation from the Free Cities or Edenvale. But why did *he* have to greet them? Garkim reflected. What was it that the emperor had actually said about this trip? *Go into the Vault of the Stone Arch, and—*

Garkim stumbled on the stairs, nearly falling in his shock. He saw the truth: Go *into* the vault, the mage-king had said! No visitor could get into that building without proper authorization, which meant the visitors were . . . they had to be . . .

Near panic, Lord Garkim ran down the remaining steps, then raced for the great hall's doors leading out to the bright morning street. The visitors were coming *through* the Stone Arch. The gate to Undermountain was opening!

Garkim ran outside, shouting for the startled grooms by the royal stables next to the ministry. A saddled horse was brought for him in just half a minute, though Garkim cursed every second of the delay. He snatched the reins, vaulted into the saddle, and with a shout was off at a gallop. Pedestrians scattered from his path as he bolted through the crowd, urging his mount toward his destination.

The gate in the Stone Arch had not been activated in decades. The visitors were coming from that buried horror of horrors, Undermountain, far to the northwest. Doegan had known little contact with the old lands of the north, but the howling depths of Undermountain, the cavern of horrors, were legendary everywhere.

Still, the mage-king had asked Lord Garkim to greet the visitors and ensure their comfort, which implied they would be friendly. As he rode for the vault, Lord Garkim sincerely hoped this was the case. Anyone coming from Undermountain would be a formidable opponent. To let such a being roam the city freely would be worse than allowing a thousand serpents into one's bed.

Chapter 2

Out of the Gate, Into the Fire

A light breeze from the sea stirred the fronds of the palm trees lining the streets outside the high-domed vault of the Stone Arch. The four guards at the top of the Vault's granite steps came to attention when they saw a sweating Lord Garkim jump from his horse, leaving it untethered in the street, and race up the steps toward them. The guard sergeant stepped forward uncertainly to challenge him.

"The password is *zal tran kor mok*!" Garkim barked, hurrying past the larger man. "Guard the entry!"

The guards backed off, looking at one another in astonishment. The guard sergeant shouted for two of their fellows down the street to join them, and they took up positions of greater alertness, their weapons drawn and readied for an unknown foe.

Ikavi spat other passwords at the guards at the second doorway, then stood impatiently as the two huge bronze doors there remained closed a little longer. His eyes took in the white pillars, the nervous soldiers, the huge solemn statues to either side of the inner door, the curling paper on the wall with its brief regulations for guarding the vault.

One of the two massive doors creaked as it slowly opened inward. No one was visible on the other side. Ikavi waited, teeth grinding, as the door opened fully. Just beyond the doorway was a huge, squat, doglike statue sitting on its haunches, in a narrow hallway that curved off to the left and right away from Garkim. The stone dog was as thick as a bull and the height of a man, its expressionless eyes looking in Lord Garkim's direction.

The dog's stone lips abruptly moved as if they were flesh. "You may pass," it said, then returned to its state of immobility.

Garkim stepped through the door and heard it slowly shut behind him. He hurried on to the left, toward the final set of doors. "The gate in the Stone Arch is opening!" he shouted.

"The arch gate is opening!" called an invisible guardsman somewhere above. Whispers and a metallic rustling echoed through the curved hall, then—nothing. Magical silence reigned.

Lord Garkim reached the far doors on the inner wall and pulled up short. "Let me pass," he said, panting from exertion.

The doors vanished. He went through the doorway, then heard a rush of air behind him. The hall through which he had passed was now sealed and trapped with magical stone and iron.

Garkim walked into a vast, bright hall, octagonal in shape, with thick, round pillars reaching along its walls to support the high dome above. Rippling colors reflected from the marble walls, nearly drowned in the sunlike brilliance of the magical light pouring down from the ceiling. Metal nails in Garkim's boot soles clacked and echoed until he came to a stop and eyed the great chamber. It appeared to be empty except for a lone object standing in the center of the room's colorful tile-mosaic floor.

Only forty feet away was a dirty gray arch carved from a single slab of rock, covered with glyphs and runes. Garkim had seen this chamber several times before on routine visits. The elaborately etched stone had not changed, nor had the "door" of rainbow light that filled the space beneath the arch. Garkim glanced at the floor, noted his location on the complex mosaic, and stepped back a pace. He allowed himself a deep sigh. He'd apparently made it in time.

The flickering rainbow curtain inside the Stone Arch faded; a ripple of darkness filled the space instead. Lord Garkim flinched. He had never seen a gate in operation. The inside of the gate was now an opaque black surface. His right hand strayed to the hilt of the long sword strapped to his belt, but he forced his hand down to his side. It would be damaging to betray fear with guards watching him from above.

Someone stepped out of the gate into the great domed chamber. It was a man, as large and broad-shouldered as a soldier of the Ffolk, in bright silver plate mail and an open-faced helm that revealed a long mustache, long dark hair, and square face. He entered leading with his bright round shield in his left hand, head down, shoving forward hard as he did so in case anyone tried to block his way. A long-handled warhammer came up in his right hand, ready for an overhand strike. Garkim had never seen armor and weaponry so elaborately engraved and decorated. A great warrior, indeed. The shield, which seemed to glow, had a balance and scales engraved upon it.

Garkim put his right hand slightly out to his side and waved back, in a warding gesture. *Do not attack*, he telepathically told the guards above. Then he opened his mind to receive the stranger's alien thoughts.

"Identify yourself!" the warrior ordered Garkim. He spoke Faerûnian Common, not the Thorass Garkim had expected, but Garkim had studied many languages. He nodded agreeably before answering. The fighter was a religious warrior and gave few second chances. The visitor stepped away from the gate, which was still black. More warriors were coming, Garkim understood.

"Be at peace!" Garkim called in Common, making no unnecessary movements. "Do not approach me. Stay near the gate. You are in—" He hesitated. A second warrior, a young man in gold-scale armor, came through the arch. This one led with his long warhammer, punching it forward to clear his way. Finding no opposition, he spotted his fellow and took up a position on the other side of the arch, both warriors swiftly scanning the room for other threats.

Garkim stifled a gasp as he received their thoughts. They were holy warriors of Tyr, the ancient god of justice! Did they know of . . . ? No—no, they were here *seeking* someone, a kidnapped woman. . . .

"You are in no danger where you stand," Garkim called out, putting strength in his voice. "Stay close to the gate and do not approach me immediately. My name is Lord Ikavi Garkim."

"Is this the Utter East?" shouted the golden warrior. Strands of carrot-red hair, damp with sweat, clung to his forehead.

Garkim noted the gate inside the arch was still black. "It is," he replied. "From where do you hail?"

"We came from Undermountain," the silver-armored warrior replied, turning his full attention to the councilor. His hammer was still ready to strike. "It would be wise to answer us truthfully. Are there traps in this room, around us?"

He can tell if I am lying. He reads my voice as I read his mind. "Yes, there are traps," said the councilor. "You are in no danger if you follow my instructions. Do not approach me."

"You said that already," said the golden warrior, looking up at the brightly lit dome far above. "We—" He stopped and turned, hearing a footfall.

A third armored warrior came through, leading with a bright two-handed sword. He glanced left and right, saw his allies, and traded places with

the first warrior at the latter's motion. Moments
later, a fourth man walked out of the blackness beneath the stone arch. He was an older man in
loose-fitting leather clothing, a long, thick staff
held out in a defensive posture before him. His
long, silver hair was tied back in a ponytail. He
stayed behind the other three, but glanced back at
the gate and moved aside.

A wizard, he is a wizard. Wait—the others don't
know what he really is. He is a secret wizard, pos-
ing as a staff-armed warrior. He hopes he will not
have to drop his disguise as a fighter. A youth and
another wizard are behind him. Garkim nodded
thoughtfully. "Are more of your party coming
through the gate?" he asked.

"Yes," said the first warrior shortly. "Now, tell us
exactly where we are."

"Certainly, certainly," said Garkim slowly, gathering the last of their thoughts. The next man through
would be a novice, a trouble-prone sort tolerated by
the others despite his clumsiness. A wizard-woman,
a noble, would be the last person to enter through
the gate. This group was bent on finding someone
here, a kidnapped woman with whom Garkim was
unfamiliar. They had already fought many powerful
monsters guarding the gate's other end in Undermountain, and they had expected to fight hundreds
more monsters here. They were astonished but still
relieved to find only a well-dressed man inside a
marble rotunda full of light—but they expected
their host to sprout fangs and wings at any second.
Garkim carefully drew a breath.

"Well?" demanded the first warrior.

"You are in a building that is called the Vault of

the Stone Arch," Garkim began. "We are in the city
of Eldrinpar, in the Imperial Reaches of Doegan.
Further greetings must wait, however. Follow my
instructions if you would leave this area safely.
Look down at the mosaic floor on which you are
standing. You must not cross the great circle of
flowers made from red and yellow tiles that you see.
Ker—" He cut himself off; he had almost used the
golden warrior's name. It wouldn't do to let them
know he could read their minds. "Keep inside that
circle, and no harm will come to you. Sir—you with
the golden armor, you are very close to the edge."

The golden warrior did not back up. "I dislike
being fenced in, my good man. What will happen if
I take another step?"

You will die, thought Garkim irritably. "You will
trigger a trap, and you will have little time in
which to regret it," he said loudly. "You are safe
there, where you are. Please lower your weapons
and pay attention to my instructions."

"Identify yourself more fully to us first," said
the silver warrior grimly. He stepped forward, his
right armored foot coming to rest a fraction of an
inch from the circle of inlaid flowers. "You seem to
have been expec—"

"Hey! Is this the Utter East?"

Startled, everyone looked back at the gate. A
clean-shaven youth with short, sandy hair and
well-tailored clothing had come through. He held
a large fighting knife out as he turned around,
staring at the chamber with huge eyes. He carried
a large backpack with a bedroll on top, and a long
coil of thin rope hung from his belt. "Wow!" he
gasped. "What a place!"

The gold-armored warrior abruptly reached out with his hammer and struck a light, glancing blow against the white tile floor outside the circle of inlaid flowers. It happened too fast for Lord Garkim to catch the thought and shout a warning. He was in the act of flinging up his arms to shield his face when the trap went off.

A block of black stone fell out of nowhere from above and struck the ground directly in front of the gold-armored warrior with a bone-jarring crash. Shattered floor tiles flew across the room, hammering armor and battering exposed skin. The gold warrior fell backward, his hammer clattering to the ground beside him. The black pillar, as wide across as a man's outstretched arms and half again the height of a tall man, settled upright into the smashed tile floor with a groan, then was silent.

"Stay where you are!" roared Garkim, enraged and unnerved. "Stay there or you will be killed!"

Several of the visitors moved anyway, grabbing the golden warrior and hauling him and his weapon away from the stone, closer to the black gate. The warrior with the staff helped the armored man to his feet.

Anger burned in Garkim's face. "The gods curse your stupidity!" he shouted in fury at the group, now bunched defensively around the arch. "This room is protected against all invaders using the gate! You are idiots and fools to doubt me!"

The visitors said nothing, their weapons ready. After a pause, however, the silver-clad warrior—their leader—lowered his shield and hammer. He exhaled and nodded his head, muttering instructions to his comrades. The men moved away from the black gate, eyeing it and Lord Garkim with grave suspicion.

"We will follow your directions, then," said the leader to Garkim. "My name is Miltiades, of Phlan. You obviously anticipated our arrival."

"Not I," said Garkim, forcing himself to be civil with an effort. "Your arrival was foreseen by my liege, our emperor, the Mage-King Aetheric III of the Imperial Reaches of Doegan, who bids you welcome. I am instructed to see you *safely* out of this building and guide you to quarters prepared for you in the mage-king's palace."

"I thought this was the Utter East, not some empire," mumbled the youngest man.

"Noph," warned the silver warrior.

"This is indeed the Utter East, or at least a part of it," said Lord Garkim. "It is well that you came here and not to one of our neighboring kingdoms, but we can discuss that later. For now, be assured that you are in good hands."

The third man through the gate, the one with curly blond hair and a two-handed sword, grinned as the tip of his weapon touched the floor. "You don't seem fond of people just coming and going through the gate," he responded. He tilted his head briefly toward the huge block of stone to the side, then glanced back at the gate. "Speaking of which, what's keeping Aleena?"

"Experience with gates breeds great caution," said Garkim. "Only a poor man or a fool fails to bar his door. Now, if you at last wish to escape this chamber, you must first look—"

He broke off and craned his neck, his gaze going past the newcomers. Something behind the visitors had changed. He hadn't yet caught what it was—he hadn't been paying attention. The newcomers, following his gaze, turned to look at the gate.

"Tyr's Word," someone whispered in shock.

Lord Garkim stared in astonishment, his instructions forgotten. The blackness inside the stone arch had vanished. No colors replaced it. He could look under the arch and see the other side of the rotunda clearly.

"The gate!" shouted the golden-armored warrior. He turned to the silver warrior in amazement. "What happened to the gate?"

The silver warrior shook his head, staring at the space under the stone arch. "That should not have happened," he muttered, glancing uneasily at Lord Garkim. "The gate should still be working, unless—"

"Unless something happened at the other end," said Kern suddenly. He stepped forward, tested the space under the stone arch with his hammer, then slapped a hand against the stone arch. The runes that covered it were dark and lifeless. "Where is Aleena? Did some fiend attack her?"

Noph cleared his throat.

"Uh, guys, it's okay," he said. Everyone turned to stare at him. The youth had already put away his knife. "Uh, Aleena, um, she stayed back. Maybe she . . ."

"She *what*?" shouted several of the men at once.

Lord Garkim closed his eyes for a moment and sighed.

It was going to be a day he would not soon forget.

Chapter 3

Of Elephants and Bloodforge Wars

Lord Garkim could read minds, but having five strong-willed subjects made the process difficult. It proved to be easier to keep all conversations with them direct and to the point. It never hurt to first play the good host, of course, as it led to a lowering of mental barriers and swift answers later.

As Garkim and the five visitors left the vault, they pushed through a growing crowd at the top of the steps by the main door, where confused guards and two city councilors talked rapidly with several of Doegan's best wizards. Garkim had nothing left to tell them, his verbal reports already made. His mission to bring the visitors back to the palace took priority even over the gate's failure.

The visitors from Undermountain remained silent in the confusion, following Garkim's lead. They had already tied down, sheathed, or peace-bonded their weapons for the trip to the palace. A royal passenger wagon harnessed to a small, short-eared elephant awaited them on the street, with a brown-skinned Mar driver brought from the royal stables. The five visitors gave the elephant long, wide-eyed looks. Several of the men rubbed their eyes in disbelief.

"Where are your horses?" Noph asked, tearing his gaze away to look up and down the crowded street. "Or do you only have monsters to pull your wagons?"

"Horses!" Lord Garkim laughed, leading the group down the steps from the vault's doors. "Alas, horses do not fare well here. A few came when this land was settled, but most died from disease. What few we have left are for important business only, not for easy rides across town. The red oxen and our eternal friends, the elephants, are far more durable. You are in no danger from this beast. It is quite intelligent and friendly."

When they reached the wagon, the newcomers crowded close to the elephant and dared to touch it. Even Miltiades was impressed. "As you might be with us for a while," said Garkim in a friendly tone, behind the group, "I will tell you more about our fair realm." He signaled, and the drover pulled down the wooden stepladder on the wagon's side. Garkim swiftly climbed aboard, seating himself on a silk-padded sideboard. "Later, I should like to discuss your own business here, of course."

Garkim already knew why the five were here, but it was always useful to know how far they would go to cover up the truth. Garkim had no illusions about lying. Everyone, even children, lied or shaded the truth. They did it almost every hour.

"We would like to hear about your kingdom first," said Miltiades. He spoke politely but made the request sound like an order. "We had an arduous journey getting to our end of the gate, and we would like to collect our thoughts while we ride." He hesitated before boarding the wagon, giving the elephant a last long look, then climbed the steps and took his seat across from Garkim.

Garkim grimaced, thinking of the damage that metallic armor would do to the wagon's silk cushions. It could not be helped, but the visitors would be happy to dump their armor by nightfall once they'd experienced a bit more of Doegan's late-summer heat and humidity.

The seat cushions were a niggling matter, though. The visitors were without a doubt quite dangerous, and Garkim had already marked Miltiades for special attention. The holy warrior's thoughts revealed he was by far the most experienced of the group, constantly sifting through hundreds of possible actions and reactions, ever alert for betrayal or attack. He was no genius, but he was far less a fool than any of his comrades, Garkim thought.

The councilor waited until the rest of the group was aboard before ordering the elephant's driver to set off. The robed driver called out a command in Maran, prodding the beast with a hooked implement. The wagon lurched forward as the elephant took up a slow, steady pace through the street past waving vendors, yoked oxen hauling carts, and endless numbers of dusty, robed citizens. The sky was clear, and the noon sun was hot.

"To begin with," Garkim said pleasantly, "we properly refer to our realm as an empire, not a kingdom." He glanced at Noph. "As things stand now, however, all of our provinces are in rebellion and have declared themselves independent, so we are technically less an empire than a kingdom. For now, at any rate. You are the guests of the Mage-King Aetheric III, Emperor of the Imperial Reaches of Doegan. This fine city is our capital, Eldrinpar. The Doegan Empire is the most powerful of all realms here, and our navy is supreme throughout the seas of what you call the Utter East. I should say that the term, 'the Utter East,' is not used much these days except perhaps by poets. We refer to our lands as the Five Kingdoms.

"Doegan and the other realms were colonized just over two hundred years ago by a fleet of Ffolk from the Moonshae Islands. You have heard of these islands, yes?" Garkim saw the five men nod and nodded himself in satisfaction, looking away again at the street scene as they rode. "This region was already long inhabited by my own people, the Mar. We are smaller and darker than the Ffolk, as you see, and my ancestors' ways were less civilized than those of the divinely blessed newcomers. The

Mar did not fare well against the conquering Ffolk in their various wars and rebellions, but eventually the two groups made peace and settled into their present civilization, which has benefited everyone."

Garkim paused. He could tell from the group's thoughts that they had already noticed that the short, brown Mar in the street around them were poverty-stricken, while the few people who had visibly pale skin were well-dressed and well-fed. He shrugged. He was so used to this that it made no impression on him. The newcomers could think what they wished.

"The original fleet from the Moonshaes was commanded by Duke Aetheric, an ancestor of our emperor, who is said to have left the Moonshaes to destroy pirates to the south. It is rumored that the duke hoped to gain enough treasure from raiding the pirates that he could pay off debts of his own, but who can say for sure? He had assembled ships from several sources in the Moonshaes—a Count Boarswic, a Lady Cambor, a Baron Parsane, some temples, and a group of Northmen in longboats. The fleet met no pirates but suffered dreadfully from the ravages of plague, which caused many ports to deny them entry, food, and treatment. The fleet was forced farther south by this and by great storms until it came to rest on the beaches of our fair land."

"Which temples went with them?" said Kern, the red-haired holy warrior in the gold-scale armor.

"Hmm." Garkim stared ahead at the high tower of the palace in the distance, weighing his reply. This could be a touchy spot. "I will consult the old writings for you concerning that point," he said slowly. "The references are confused on this. Tempus and the Earthmother, certainly, were among them and are with us now." He cleared his throat and resumed. "As I was saying, the ships dropped anchor here, and the various groups held council to decide what they should do. Conflict swiftly broke out between them, and each group finally elected to go its own way.

"They called this place the Utter East and formed five different kingdoms. Duke Aetheric became the king of Doegan, Lady Cambor queen of Edenvale, Count Boarswic king of the debased and degenerate realm of Konigheim, and the Northmen settled their own rough spot, which they called the Mead-Hall of Clan Chief Harvald. Baron Parsane and his ship were tragically lost on the voyage over, but the crews of his surviving ships established the Free Cities of Parsanic, which are as chaotic a group as you could hope to deal with. Best for you that the gate led you here. 'Tis a pity it . . . ceased to function."

They are thinking of the wizard-woman they left at the other gate, back in Undermountain, Garkim thought. Aleena Paladinstar was her name. The boy has feelings for her. Garkim rolled his eyes.

"Aleena must have done it," interjected Noph with a gloomy look. "She said she wasn't coming. I'll, uh, explain later."

Miltiades stared at his young companion, then shrugged. "Very well. Lord Garkim, please continue with your story. What happened to the temples' ships?"

"The temples' ships . . . The representatives of the temples were denied a vote in the fleet's last council. One high priest had been killed by a sea monster before landing, and many priests were dispirited and had lost their powers. They settled among the Ffolk in the various colonies. Many of these former priests gained power in an evil cult later, but that's another story."

Jacob, the warrior with the two-handed sword, cleared his throat. "Perhaps we might be of assistance in rooting out these wretches, if—"

"Let Lord Garkim continue," interrupted Miltiades. "We have other business to which we must attend."

There was an embarrassed silence. "Your pardon," said Jacob, subdued.

"Your offer of assistance is appreciated," said Garkim diplomatically. He paused, listening to the steady thump of the elephant's feet and the creaking of the wagon's wheels over the hard-packed earth of the street. The visitors were considering ways to find out where this kidnapped woman they sought was held, he knew. All in good time, all in good time. The mage-king obviously had something in mind for these gentlemen first.

"To continue," Garkim went on, "the various colonies were settled, and the Mar, the inhabitants of this fertile land, came to an accommodation with the inv—with the Ffolk. The—"

"Were you going to say, 'invaders'?" The voice was Noph's, from where he perched at the rear of the jostling wagon, holding on to his seat with both hands.

Garkim burst out laughing. "In fact, I was, yes.

There are many points of view on this, and sometimes it is best not to take sides too obviously. You understand. The past is the past."

"It looks like the past is still with you," responded Noph. He was looking behind the wagon at a cluster of beggars following them at a safe distance, hands outstretched beneath pleading faces.

Garkim's smile faded as he read Noph's thoughts. "Ah, yes. It is with us, you are right. It is everywhere, the past. But this is now, and we must deal with what is now. To understand the now, I will explain a bit more about the past and bring you to the present.

"The Founding Lords, the Ffolk who landed on these shores, explored this new realm. They investigated the old ruins that dot our land, meddled in sacred tribal lands, hunted for gold and whatever valuables they could pull from overgrown tombs. They were like puppies, digging for their treasures, but they were not wise—or so some of my people say. The Ffolk built their kingdoms, and this much was well and good, you see, but the digging into old ruins—this is dangerous even in your home lands, is it not?"

There was a general murmur of agreement at this from the others. Garkim nodded. They came here from Undermountain, after all. He mulled over what he would say next. He should tell them about the bloodforges, he knew. The mage-king had not forbidden it, and they would hear about bloodforges soon enough from any citizen of the kingdom. Still—the short version would do.

"A hundred years ago," he went on, "an explorer

from Edenvale looted an old temple and found a great glowing stone. It was so large that he had to bring it back in a wagon, but the queen made him rich and had her wizards and priests set to work probing its secrets. In time, they discovered some of its powers, and they named this stone the bloodforge."

Several of the men gasped audibly. "The bloodforge!" he heard Noph whisper. "That's what we came here to—"

"Shhh!" several men responded at once.

"You said the queen of Edenvale had her priests study this device, the bloodforge," spoke Miltiades loudly, trying to drown out the whispering. "Were these the same evil priests you talked of earlier?"

"No, no, they were not. A large number of priests had come on the voyage, and most are still honored in our kingdom today, though most of my own people, the Mar, prefer the original gods who held sway here. You understand, of course."

"Any worshipers of Righteous Tyr around?" asked Kern with considerable eagerness.

Garkim's mouth twitched. Careful. . . . "No, I am afraid not," he said at last. "The worship of many gods known to the Moonshaes was never brought over by the fleet at the start."

Kern sighed heavily. "That is grave news," he said, with honest regret.

Garkim decided not to comment further. "Be that as it may, I must explain the role of the bloodforges in subsequent events. The queen of Edenvale learned to use the powers of this device to conjure up magical beings, sufficient to create an army of unthinking and loyal troops. This was power unheard of, as you can imagine, and she put it to use at once against her rival, the king of Konigheim."

"Count Boarswic, you mean," offered Kern. "You didn't seem very fond of his kingdom when you spoke of it earlier."

Garkim gave a long mental sigh and lightly brushed his temples with his fingertips. Deep in the back of his head he could feel the beginning of a dull pain. One of his headaches was coming. "I believe the king of Konigheim at this time was Brand the Slaver King, as the first Boarswic had died long before. This was a hundred years after the settling of this land by the fleet. The queen of Edenvale then was Rosamund Flame-Hair. And yes, I am not fond of Konigheim, nor is anyone fond of Konigheim who is sane and a lover of life and law. To this day they kidnap our border citizens and sell them off farther north into slavery, though we repeatedly make them regret such doings. But I digress."

Garkim felt a surge of anxiety from the men before him. The visitors were now wondering if the kidnapped woman they sought had been sold into slavery in just this manner. It was possible, admitted Garkim to himself, but of no importance for now—except to them. Garkim made a note to check on this later.

"Rosamund and Brand fought, and Brand's forces failed. They could not prevail against the army Rosamund's bloodforge had brought forth. Then Brand found a bloodforge of his own. He conquered Rosamund's forces and took her bloodforge, too. But he was himself murdered by his own family—a common thing in Konigheim. While Brand's kingdom fell into civil war, the forces of Edenvale's royal consort, the dead queen's husband, discovered another bloodforge. Then the Northmen found the fourth, and finally our own King Helvar found the fifth. As was his right by decree of the gods and his ancestor Aetheric's command of the fleet that brought the Ffolk to these shores, King Helvar declared himself emperor of the Five Kingdoms and set out forcibly bringing order to the land. He was unsuccessful, but his example continues to inspire us in the present day."

"What do these other kingdoms think about having you bring order to them?" The casual question came from the visitor who had not yet spoken—the secret wizard, Trandon.

The question, though expected, was irksome. "They are not fond of the idea, of course," said Garkim briskly, "but it is a shame, as the disorder and chaos has produced terrible grief in this land. The Free Cities of Parsanic, which know little of true responsibility and all too much of their selfish freedom, gained the services of one of the warring factions in Konigheim, which had its own bloodforge. At this point, each of the five Founding Lords' states had a bloodforge, and I can cover in full the events of the following decade merely by saying that we were perpetually at war, all the Five Kingdoms, though it cost very few lives. The bloodforges conjured whole armies with a few moments' work, once their secrets were understood. A few real, live persons died now and then in the raiding, to be sure, but for the most part we were spared the horrors usually visited on kingdoms engaged in such activities."

A short silence followed as the five visitors digested this bit of history. Kern spoke next. "Everyone finally sickened of this sport in the end?"

Garkim considered the proper response. "Indeed. It became all too apparent in time that use of the bloodforges had a price, one that was not evident when they were found. They rendered changes in the blood and bone of those who used them, which . . . um . . ." He hesitated. He had not had to explain this in many years. His diplomatic tongue failed for a moment and his headache increased.

He decided to backtrack. "Those who used the bloodforges were changed in many ways that soon reduced their appetite for using these ancient devices. Equally troubling, it was also discovered that the bloodforges somehow attracted the attention of monsters, and the more often the bloodforges were used, the more monsters appeared and the more trouble these monsters brought. Our kingdoms have largely been at peace for the last seven decades, thanks in great part to the foresight of Mage-King Aetheric II, long may he live in memory, who discovered the connection between the coming of the beasts and usage of the bloodforges. He raised up true armies again, which had nearly vanished except for palace and personal guards, and he made Doegan a realm with real might, a sanctuary and haven against a tide of darkness."

"So there are no more monsters around," finished Kern.

Garkim hesitated. "I did not say that," he responded at last, as the drover called an order to the elephant and the wagon creaked to a stop. "Ah! We are almost at the palace; the drawbridge is around the corner ahead, to the right. We must dismount here and cross over the bridge by foot. You can admire our little Eldrin River, which was rechanneled by King Erwain, son of Aetheric I, to serve as a moat. A lovely job he did, too."

The drover had the wooden steps down in a second. As he climbed down, Garkim noted that the five visitors were eyeing each other and had made no move yet to get up. They were also sweating profusely from the heat. He smiled to himself. "You are in no danger from monsters here," he added casually, handing the drover a few coins, drawing the man's startled thanks. "It is unlikely you will be troubled at all during your stay, in fact. Doegan is as safe as your own homes." He casually waved a hand toward the corner. "Please come with me."

Exhaling heavily, Miltiades got up, moved to the steps, and climbed down to the ground. A moment later, every other man did the same. Garkim then turned and led the group to the corner and the drawbridge beyond.

Miltiades didn't trust him, Garkim knew, but that was to be expected. The other four men assumed that they were indeed safe here, and they meant to set about their errand of mercy without further delay. They planned to find this kidnapped woman, Lady Eidola, at all costs. They even had a necklace that would detect her presence. That was certainly well and good, and Garkim wished them success, if only to speed their eventual departure. After the mage-king had finished whatever use he had for them, of course.

But they had another goal in mind, to find out what power was blocking all attempts to magically spy on this city from afar, then destroy it. That could be a source of real trouble. Every one of the five men suspected that a bloodforge was responsible for this magical shielding, and every one believed he might have to find and destroy that bloodforge as a result.

This would mean the death of every one of them. Perhaps this accounted for the mage-king's interest in the group.

Garkim sighed and surreptitiously massaged his aching head. He wondered if he had told the visitors too much about the bloodforges. Or, perhaps, too little. Should he have told them that the price for use of the bloodforge extended to the entire population of the Five Kingdoms? That his ever-increasing headaches were only one symptom of a physical weakening that year by year spread wider and wider in Doegan, among Mar and Ffolk alike? It was, he reflected wryly, the supreme irony of the Utter East: as the populace grew weaker, the rulers relied more heavily on the bloodforges to keep the armies of the fiends at bay. But every use of the bloodforge weakened the population still more, continuing the vicious cycle.

No point in worrying about it for now. He led the men over the drawbridge and into the palace, drawing up plans with every step.

Chapter 4

No Rest for the Wary

Lord Garkim and his five charges were greeted
at the palace entrance by a delegation of curious
fellow councilors, all of whom had been present at
the meeting two hours earlier when Garkim was
summoned by the emperor. The councilors welcomed the overheated visitors and introduced
themselves. The weariness of the visitors and
their filthy, sweat-drenched condition were duly

noted. Chambermaids were dispatched to fix up a large guest room for the warriors, and a midafternoon luncheon was promised. The visitors seemed rather distant but appropriately pleased at such treatment.

The warm, stuffy room to which the five men were taken was an octagonal chamber about forty feet across. A broad crystal dome replaced the ceiling, revealed a bright blue sky above; brilliant flowers and long green vines hung from brass pots suspended from the ceiling by thin chains. The furniture in the room was made from a rich, dark wood, the thatched seats and backs of rough fibers dyed in colorful striped patterns. Long silk tapestries hung from the rough stone walls. The floor was covered by a thick carpet whose colorful pattern had faded from exposure to sunlight from above as well as the scuffing of shoes.

The five men looked about the room cautiously as they entered, but saw nothing amiss. As the maids left, a well-dressed Mar servant pointed out the side bedrooms that led off from six of the room's eight walls. The entry door and a bookcase with assorted knickknacks and small volumes took up the last two walls.

Miltiades nodded his thanks to the servant, who closed the door behind him as he left. The old warrior silently eyed the other members of his group. Rivers of sweat ran down his face.

Noph tried the handle to one of the doors, then pushed the door open and peered inside. "Huh," he said. "Nice place. Maybe there's a fan here somewhere."

Miltiades carefully removed his helmet and

tucked it under his arm. He tried the door to the left of the entrance to the room and looked inside. He sniffed after giving it a quick examination. "It is fine, as bedrooms go," he said, turning about. "I suggest we make ourselves presentable while we discuss our plans. Whatever our mission, we are always representatives of Tyr. Let us never forget that." He entered his chosen room and peered into a mirror on the wall.

"What he means," said Jacob mischievously, "is that it will never do to face death and not look your best."

Kern chuckled as he looked himself over. "So true," he said. "I suppose I could use a bath, and the armor a little polish. But business first." He reached up and tugged at something at his throat. A moment later he held up a quarter-inch-wide ball of crystal, a pendant on a thin gold chain. "Hmm. It would seem that Lady Eidola is not within a mile of us at the moment. Unless . . ." He carefully took off the pendant and held it out to Jacob, who took it in his hand. The crystal pendant remained as it was.

"She's definitely not around," Kern said, discouraged. "Sometimes magical things don't work when they touch me, because my body is so anti-magical." He took back the necklace, then sighed and rubbed his face with a thick hand. "If she's not here, this is bad news. We'd better start thinking now about ways to find and rescue our lady."

"Find the nearest bloodforge," suggested Trandon in a low voice. He stood across the room by the bookcase, peering at the books on the shelves.

"Well," said Jacob, doffing his own helmet and

running a hand through his blond curls. "That would be mage-king Aetheric's, now wouldn't it? Shall we just ask to see it, or should we fight our way in?"

"Don't be facetious," said Kern darkly. "We could really use Aleena's help about now. Noph, what was that you said earlier, about Aleena not wanting to come along?"

Noph blinked. "Oh. She said . . . she said . . ." He paused, then continued, "She said she had several reasons." He straightened his shoulders. "I'm sure they must have been important."

Miltiades's voice rumbled out from his room, an angry edge to it. "Aleena *may* have had good reasons to stay behind, but I do not see why she could not have told me what they were. Why should she have confided in you and not me? I do not entirely trust the sorceress."

Noph's mouth fell open. "Not trust . . . ! But she's Aleena Paladinstar. She's a friend of the Blackstaff!"

From his room Miltiades snorted. "To my thinking that makes her less trustworthy, not more. In any event, she is not here, and the way we came is now destroyed."

The other men in the room looked away from Noph. Jacob nodded soberly. "This does present a problem when we're finally ready to go home," he said.

"Or ready to communicate with anyone outside this city," said Miltiades. He came out of his room. In his right hand was a small jeweled mirror. "I speak with my wife Evaine in Phlan using this device, but I cannot do it now. Something is blocking the magical link between this mirror and Phlan, probably the same force that prevents Khelben from scrying on this city."

"I'll tell you what else bothers me," said Jacob, wandering over to another side door as Miltiades went back into his room.

"That they knew we were coming," said Trandon, not looking up from a book he had picked out.

"Exactly," said Jacob, seizing the door's handle and pushing it open. "That is exactly it. I'd love to—Great Tyr!"

Jacob was not fast enough to dodge the blow he saw coming. It knocked him back into the room and sent him crashing into a chair, which broke into pieces under his armored weight.

Kern reacted instantly, seizing his warhammer and tearing it free of his belt. He knocked aside another chair to get to Jacob, ready for battle. Trandon dropped his book and snatched his staff. Miltiades came out of his room again, shield and hammer in his hands but missing his helmet. Noph was too startled to do more than stand and watch.

From the doorway Jacob had tried to enter stepped a tall, bald, bare-chested man. He stooped to pass through the seven-foot doorframe. His skin was a maroon red, the color of dark clay, but he was far larger and more broadly built than any normal human. To Noph, staring in amazement, he seemed more than eight feet tall, with enormous muscles that properly belonged on a wild beast. A little giant, Noph thought.

Seeing that Jacob was merely stunned, Kern charged the huge red man. He swung his hammer in a roundhouse blow.

The red man caught the hammerhead in the palm of one enormous hand with a loud slap. He twisted and pulled at the same moment, throwing Kern off balance and dragging the hammer from his grasp. Kern flew past him with a cry and crashed into Trandon and the bookcase beside him, breaking the case and spilling old volumes and wooden objects everywhere.

Miltiades moved in swiftly, but did not close with the red giant. Jacob crawled back, trying to tug free his two-handed sword from his over-the-shoulder scabbard. The bald red giant studied Miltiades silently with eyes so dark they appeared black. Then he dropped Kern's warhammer to the carpet and lunged at the warrior.

Miltiades threw his shield up and stepped to one side, out of the giant's line of movement. The giant punched down at the same moment, his massive fist striking a glancing blow to the shield but knocking Miltiades back a step. The old warrior suddenly lashed out and slammed his hammer into the giant's nearest leg, exactly at the kneecap.

The blow snapped the giant's leg backward, breaking the knee joint with a loud crack that made Noph's heart jump. The giant fell heavily, flattening a table and chair beneath him. Miltiades moved sideways but caught a foot in the carpeting and fell himself, legs tangled.

The giant rolled, never uttering a word, and got up on his hands and one good knee. His face held no expression. He reached for Jacob, who stood nearest, his two-handed sword now free. Jacob saw the great hand reaching for him and swung down at it. His sword slashed through a hanging flowerpot overhead, ruining his attack and splattering dirt, flowers, and leaves everywhere. His attack momentum gone, Jacob tried to recover and strike again. He was too slow.

The giant caught the fighter by one arm and threw him sideways like a rag doll. Jacob crashed into a side door, knocking it off its hinges as he fell into the room beyond. His sword flew through the air, bounced off the ceiling, and clattered to the floor in front of an astonished Noph.

Trandon suddenly came at the giant, a long wall hanging in his hands. The silver-haired man whipped the hanging against the giant's head, flipping it over his face. Trandon pulled back and twisted the ends of the hanging, hoping to blind the giant for a few precious moments.

The red giant flailed his arms, missing Trandon by a hair, but the old man was forced to release the wall hanging. He stepped back and bumped solidly against the wall where the bookcase had stood.

Now free of the wall hanging, the giant turned his attention to Trandon. He got up on his good knee, facing his foe. He swiftly leaned forward, left hand out to catch one of Trandon's limbs.

Suddenly the giant made an odd gasping sound. His hand slammed into Trandon's chest and knocked the wind from him, crushing the old man against the wall. The giant looked surprised, perhaps even puzzled. Then he fell forward, face down on the floor. Trandon fell next to him, clutching his chest and trying to breathe.

Jacob's two-handed sword projected from the giant's back. Only a three-foot length of the five-foot blade was visible.

Noph stepped back, unable to believe what he had done. He looked at his hands, then back at the motionless giant. The groans of his companions failed to distract him.

"That was for you, Harloon," he said, then swallowed. He thought of his friend, a warrior who had died only hours ago back in Undermountain, his head crushed by an ettin's club. Noph looked down at the stained sleeves of his shirt, still spattered with dried drops of Harloon's blood.

"Tyr bless you, boy," said Miltiades with feeling. The warrior had finally gotten to his feet, only to see that the fight was over. He looked around at the wreckage of the room. "Next time, however, act a bit sooner. You'll make a poor warrior if you stand watching a fight with your mouth hanging open." He sighed. "Let's help our friends now, lad."

Noph nodded dully and did as he was told.

* * * * *

The five had suffered nothing worse in their fight than a few cracked ribs and many extremely painful bruises. Miltiades and Kern, being paladins, were able to heal the more serious wounds by laying on hands and praying. Their prayers were heard and answered, and within a half hour of the fight's start, they were on their feet and feeling very stiff. Everyone but Noph, who felt fine. Kern looked around and spotted Trandon. "What are you reading now?"

"An interesting book," said Trandon. He flipped a page, then closed the volume and dropped it gently on the floor among the ruins of the bookcase. "It is a history of these lands. It says what our host said earlier, but adds a few things. There were five separate temples that joined the fleet that colonized this region. One temple turned rogue and was cast out; the other temples went on to become established here."

"Which temple was that, the rogue one?" asked Kern.

"I don't know. It appears to be the one now called the Fallen Temple. The other temples were to the Earthmother"—he grimaced—"Waukeen, Tempus, and . . . Umberlee."

"Umberlee." Kern shook his head again. "That's wonderful. The Sea Bitch, down here with Waukeen's gold grubbers and Tempus's war crazies. Things are getting better all the time."

"Hey!" shouted Jacob. "Get back!"

Everyone turned, startled. There was a fog in the air over the giant's body. Jacob, who had been examining the giant, now quickly waved everyone away from it.

"The sword wound wasn't bleeding," he explained hastily, staring down at the body. "I was trying to find out if this thing was a golem, when it began to smoke. Look!"

Before their eyes, the giant's body slowly sagged. The muscles seemed to deflate, and the bones bent and curved as if they were rubber. The men armed themselves swiftly, but there was nothing to fight. Within minutes, the giant's body had decayed into a flat translucent mass of brown matter that reminded Noph of apple butter. This material gave off an odorless smoke as it shrank in size, until it had completely vanished.

Speechless, Kern toed the area of carpet where the giant's body had been just ten minutes ago. Not even a stain was left.

"What was it that Lord Garkim said?" asked Jacob. "We're as safe here as in our own homes?"

"I'd like to hear what he has to say about this," muttered Kern. "They had maids in here right up to the moment we came in. I saw one come out of this very room. This creature couldn't have been here, unless he was invisible."

"Or unless a bloodforge created him," said Trandon. Everyone looked at him. He raised an eyebrow in response. "They can create soldiers out of thin air, remember?"

"We will say nothing at all about this," said Miltiades abruptly and firmly. "We will say nothing at all. Anyone who mentions it to us will thus reveal his guilt. We are going to clean this mess up and move the debris into one of the side rooms. We will tell them we moved the furniture a bit; if they press us, we will apologize for the damage and offer payment, but say nothing about the giant. Trandon, take the books into your room if you wish to study them further. Let us act quickly." He glanced at Noph, who was still staring at the carpet where the golem had dissolved. "Come, lad, stop mooning about. There's work to be done." He pulled a gauntlet and vambrace from his arm and tossed them on the floor in front of the youth. "Polish the armor. We will need to appear at our best when next we meet Lord Garkim."

The men fell to their work. "I suppose in a way we should all be flattered," said Jacob wryly, carting off the remains of a chair. "Whoever is after us certainly thinks enough of us to send their very best."

Chapter 5

Questions and Answers

The smell of the ocean was in the afternoon air when the five bruised and battered visitors heard a knock on their door. They arose, weapons readied, but it was only Lord Garkim in the hall. He wore a wide-sleeved red silk shirt, blue dress trousers, and polished black boots. A white tabard was belted over this, a colorful blue sailing ship embroidered over his chest.

"Gentlemen, your meal is ready," said the councilor, bowing at the waist. "I thought I would come and show you the way myself."

"We are grateful for your attention," responded Miltiades, returning the bow. He led the group out of the room. Their armor was reasonably well-polished, thanks to Noph, though each thought his own armor stank to the high heavens. Better this, however, than being caught unarmored and unprepared.

Garkim led the five visitors through two grand halls, on which assorted portraits of kings and battlefields hung. Tilted shafts of sunlight fell from windows and skylights overhead. Brown-skinned maids in red-and-white dresses stopped and lowered their eyes as the procession passed, then scurried away, wondering why the knights did not doff their armor like sensible people.

Garkim said little except to greet the councilors and soldiers he met on the way. He appeared to ignore his visitors, but he picked up their thoughts and learned of their encounter with the red giant. Garkim thought it had all the earmarks of a blood-forge assassination; he could easily guess who was behind the attack, but that was for the mage-king to handle later. Meanwhile he was puzzled that the visitors made no overt mention of the attack.

Noph gave a nervous smile at Ffolk and Mar alike as he passed. He made a mental note to wash carefully when he could. Some of the Ffolk here had some sort of rash or fungus on their necks and arms. The heat and humidity were no doubt to blame. He then mulled over the fight with the red giant. He was proud of himself, but at the same time he felt a slow anger with the paladins, especially with Miltiades. He'd saved them and what was his reward? Polishing sweaty armor. If only Aleena could have seen him in the fight. He wondered what the lovely spellcaster was doing at this moment, hoping she herself was unharmed.

The dining hall was not huge, by Waterdeep standards, but it was respectable enough. The air smelled of a light burnt incense that made Noph's nose itch; it was pleasant and annoying at the same time. The central table was covered with an elaborately stitched cloth showing a procession of fantastic animals and monsters, and subdued curtains and royal paintings dominated the dark wood-plank walls.

Serving girls showed each armored man to a seat (heavily built, fortunately) and placed a small cup of red liquid in front of him before hurrying away. Garkim took the seat at the head of the table, Miltiades and Kern on his right and left. Miltiades placed his shield against a wall before he sat down. Noph sat the farthest away from Garkim, on the other side of Jacob from Kern. He picked up his cup and smelled it, then took a large sip. He abruptly choked and coughed, spitting a shower of red droplets all over himself and the tablecloth before him.

"Our wine sometimes has that effect," said Garkim, as if nothing had happened. "It is rather strong and has a few local fruits and spices added to it during the fermentation process. I will inquire about the identity of the spices, if you wish."

"It is not necessary," said Miltiades, watching Jacob thump Noph on the back. He sighed and carefully picked up his own cup, sniffing the bouquet. The wine certainly *was* unusual, very much an acquired taste: quite bitter and strong, but not poisonous. His ring would have told him if it was harmful. A gift from his wife, the ring could detect poison within one yard of the wearer—a most useful and thoughtful present, indeed.

"We are having sea fowl this afternoon," said Garkim. "It was a traditional dish of my people, before the Ffolk came. To our amazement, the Ffolk made the dish even better. It is not as spicy as it formerly was, but I hope you will find it palatable."

Kern caught Miltiades's gaze, asking a silent question. The paladin leader shrugged. Kern lifted his own cup and swished its red contents around. "Your lordship," he began, "I have a few questions about your kingdom that I hope you can answer. We knew next to nothing about this land when we arrived here, and we are all quite curious about your realm. We don't wish to bruise your hospitality by doing so."

Lord Garkim smiled. His white teeth flashed. "I will be all answers, good sir, but I have some questions for you of my own. I have told you much about our fair and fortunate land, but I know next to nothing about your homeland, or yourselves—or the mission that brought you here." He waited expectantly.

The men at the table traded looks. Miltiades took a deep breath. "We came here from Waterdeep, a great city far to the northwest. We were sent on a quest to recover a noble woman from Waterdeep, Lady Eidola, who was kidnapped and taken away." He paused for a second or two. "The kidnappers made their escape through a gatelike spell, something similar to that archway through which we arrived. We were able to determine that the gate led directly to this region. We suspect it led, in fact, to this city."

Miltiades stared directly into the councilor's eyes. The councilor stared back without blinking.

"There is the possibility that your belief as to the destination of the kidnappers was mistaken, perhaps," said Garkim, without inflection.

"No chance whatsoever," said the paladin quietly.

"Ah." The councilor nodded, still not breaking his gaze. "Explain to me, if you will, why you think this lady—Eidola, is it?—to be within the walls of Eldrinpar."

"The mage Khelben Arunsun, the Blackstaff, foremost mage of Waterdeep, scried the Utter East, looking for the Lady Eidola," Miltiades replied. "His scrying magic failed to see the other side of the portal from Undermountain to the Utter East. Thus he believes Eidola must be somewhere in that area to which his magic cannot penetrate. In other words, within this city."

Garkim was silent a moment. "This is grave news," he said. "Would you describe this lady for me, please?"

Miltiades thought, his posture relaxing. "Lady Eidola has long auburn hair and silver-gray eyes. Her skin is pale, like ours, but tanned from the sun. She has many freckles across her nose and upper cheeks. She would be about a hand's width taller than yourself, well muscled, high spirited. She was . . . she was wearing a long, white wedding dress when she was taken. She was taken away on her wedding day, before the ceremony was completed."

Garkim shook his head in sympathy. "She was to be your wife?" he asked.

Several of the men instantly shook their heads and said "no" at the same time. "No," said Miltiades as well. "She was to be the wife of a great lord and warrior of Waterdeep, Piergeiron Paladinson. Her loss has crippled him and disrupted the city. We are his allies and have vowed to find her."

Lord Garkim appeared shocked. "That is outrageous. I can hardly believe someone from our city would have done this evil deed, but Doegan has many enemies who would be too willing to make it appear that this city is guilty of harboring such criminals. I will have to see tomorrow what resources we can make available to you in completing your quest."

Miltiades reflected on this latter point and seemed on the verge of saying something more, but stopped. Serving maids had arrived through the doorway behind Garkim with plates of fruit. The conversation halted until the women were gone.

"So," Lord Garkim said, settling back into his seat, "you say that your only purpose here is to rescue this unhappy woman?"

His words had their desired effect. The five men traded tense looks. Miltiades spoke quickly. "We are saying that we are sworn not to return until we have found her," he said with feeling.

"Ah," said Garkim, with curious satisfaction. He seemed to have expected that answer. "Then you will return to your home in Waterdeep with her when this is over."

"Well, my home is in Phlan, a great city east of

Waterdeep," corrected Kern, happy to change the topic. "Miltiades and I are both from there. Trandon, across from me, is from Cormyr, and my buddy Jacob . . . Jacob is from everywhere, to hear him tell it, anyway." He grinned at his comrade, sitting to his left. "Only our young friend, Freeman Kastonoph, at the end here, is from Waterdeep."

"You must be greatly trusted and highly experienced to have been called upon to undertake this mission," said Garkim, making it a statement of fact. "Have you considered how you will return home when your work here is completed? I am not trying to hurry you, you must understand." He waved at the table. "We have a meal, after all. But the matter of the loss of the Stone Arch gate . . ."

Miltiades selected a bright yellow apple from the plate of fruit before him, rotating it in his fingers. It was flawless. He could see his reflection in the polished skin. "We will have to explore our options," he admitted. "The loss of the gate was not anticipated by ourselves, either. We harbor no wish to impose on your hospitality for long." He put the apple down and looked at his comrades.

Jacob took the cue. He leaned forward in his seat. "Now that we're all comfortable, I wondered if you could tell us how your emperor—um, I apologize, your lordship, but in the rush I seem to have forgotten his—"

"Mage-King Aetheric III," said both Miltiades and Garkim at the same moment. They looked at each other with raised eyebrows.

Jacob laughed. "Yes, Mage-King Aetheric III . . . I was wondering how he knew we were coming. We didn't announce our mission, of course, as we did not wish to draw attention. You understand."

Garkim smiled. "Obviously, he is a wizard king. We do not have many wizards in our land, and certainly few of his ability. He surprises all in Doegan, almost every day. We have become rather accustomed to being surprised, I fear. When he told me you were coming, I was taken aback, as no one has come though the Stone Arch in many years. But that the emperor would know of your coming—" He raised his hands in mock surrender and smiled. "As I've said, we have grown used to that sort of thing."

"Your king has a bloodforge?" asked Noph, about to bite into an orange he had peeled.

The atmosphere at the table changed in a second. Somewhere, several of those present tensed simultaneously. Noph sensed it, and was suddenly terrified he'd said something wrong, something disastrous.

Lord Garkim stared down the table at Noph. His smile was wooden, and he dropped his words into the heavy silence. "Why, yes. I said earlier that he did. The mage-king has a bloodforge, as does every ruler of the Five Kingdoms."

"Would the bloodforge give him the power to foretell our coming?" asked Kern, stepping into the breach. His smile was gone.

Garkim's smile vanished as well. "It is well within reason," he replied. The silence resumed; plainly Garkim did not relish further discussion along these lines.

"Would it be possible," Miltiades said carefully, "for your emperor to use his bloodforge in such a manner as to magically cloak this city or this kingdom, so that no one outside it could spy upon it?"

Garkim stared at Miltiades and blinked several times. "What an interesting question," he said at last. He looked as if he was about to laugh, but the laughter would not come. "You can understand that the answer to that would be of great interest to many powers who were not friendly to us, and they might wish to gain that answer to benefit themselves but do great harm to us. Why do you ask me this, if you do not mind my question?"

Miltiades looked thoughtful. "As I have told you, before our arrival we were able to determine that this city is warded in such a way that it cannot be spied upon. You must understand that we made every attempt to locate Lady Eidola, and except for this we would have never considered such an area of inquiry. Lady Eidola's loss, however, has thrown Waterdeep into great chaos. Her recovery is paramount to that great city's future, perhaps even to its survival. As a result, we came here ourselves to seek her. Were you in our position, I believe you would have done the same."

Had I been in the same position as you, Garkim thought, I would have found the missing woman by now and slain her kidnappers as well. He took a short breath. "Of course," he said, "of course. Your actions are understandable." He looked down at the tablecloth as if looking through it into the infinite distance beyond it. "I will consult with my liege this evening and discuss your mission with him. You must understand that—"

"Lord Garkim." The voice came from nowhere and filled the room, vibrating bone and wood.

Miltiades and Kern were out of their seats in a second. Kern's chair fell over backwards. Both gripped their warhammers as they looked about, ready to tear them free of their belt straps. Trandon, too, was half out of his chair, one hand frozen in the act of reaching inside the tooled leather vest he wore over his light armor. Only Garkim, Noph, and Jacob remained seated, the latter two swiveling around with wide eyes to locate the speaker.

"Yes, Your Majesty," responded Garkim, a moment after the noise died down.

"Bring the visitors to us in one half-hour," finished the voice. The five visitors looked but saw no one else in the room with them, not even a floating mouth or other phantasm.

"As you wish, Your Majesty." Garkim waited for further instructions, but none were forthcoming. "Well," he said, looking around the table, "perhaps His Majesty can clear up these matters for you in person. We will miss the sea fowl, however, which is a shame. We may as well finish the fruit."

"We are prepared to see the mage-king now," said Miltiades in a hard voice.

"It would accomplish nothing," Garkim said, unruffled. "He would take no notice of you even if you held your hammers in front of his face. You must be familiar with wizards in your own lands. Are not some of them like that?"

"Your Majesty!" shouted Miltiades. He turned, eyes up, his warhammer lowered until his fingers held it at his side. "Your Majesty!" he shouted at the walls of the room.

There was nothing but silence.

"His attention is elsewhere," said Garkim with

a sigh. He picked up a grape and ate it. "He is quite prompt about responding otherwise."

Kern lowered his warhammer as well. He knelt down and picked up his chair, setting it upright but not taking his seat yet. "A fine way to say hello," he muttered.

Garkim smiled slightly. "One gets accustomed to it."

Noph noticed that his hands were trembling. He swallowed and locked his fingers together on the tabletop to calm them. "Can—" he started to say, but stopped himself hastily.

Garkim caught his gaze. "You may go on," he said.

Noph glanced at the others, then licked his lips. "I was wondering . . . does the mage-king have . . . can he hear what we are saying?"

"That is entirely possible," said Garkim easily, "though I don't believe he is doing so now. He uses his sorcery to investigate various places around our kingdom and particularly our city, but it is difficult to say whether he hears *everything* that is said by his subjects, or sees everything they do, even within his own palace. He has so many things on his mind lately, it is impossible to know what he is doing. In the meanwhile, I say again that we have a few minutes before we meet him. It would not hurt to eat."

Miltiades nodded and slowly took his seat again, eyes fixed on the tabletop. He picked up the yellow apple before him and regarded it solemnly. "Enough questions for now, then," he said. "Let us enjoy our repast, then speak with the mage-king. I am sure we will have much to talk about." He bit into the apple, devouring his reflection whole.

Chapter 6

An Empty Throne Room

Shortly, Lord Garkim led the five visitors on another journey down two more halls, passing great windows overlooking gardens, portraits in faded oils, skylights and crystal chandeliers, and other palace finery. Thick rugs muffled their tread. The air smelled of sea spray, and the endless roar of waves whispered in the distance.

At the end of the final corridor was an ornate

set of double doors, each of dark, polished wood and half again the height of a man. Two guards stood at ease there, one before each door, each holding a poleaxe upright in one hand.

"On *guard*," said the man on the left, spotting Garkim. The two came to attention.

"The Councilor of Internal Investigations, Lord Ikavi Garkim, and five visitors, here to see the Emperor, His Majesty, the Mage-King Aetheric III," responded Garkim, loudly and clearly.

The two guards stepped apart, putting their backs to the walls on either side of the double doors. Garkim nodded to the men, each a head taller than he and light-skinned, and he walked past them to the door. He caught hold of an elaborate brass handle on one door and turned to face the knights.

"Gentlemen," he said, and he opened the door for them. Beyond was a vast, darkened hall whose floor was made of flat, fitted stone.

Miltiades's face betrayed astonishment. "Is this all the guard your king has?" he asked. His right hand caught the shaft of his hammer and gripped it lightly. The other four men saw this and stopped, unsure of what was going on.

"It is all the guard the king needs," said Garkim with an edge to his voice. "If you suspect a trap, I am more than willing to enter first. That would be a grave breach of protocol, of course, but if it would ease your fears . . ."

The old knight glared at the smaller man. He then strode first into the dark chamber. The great room was flooded with light as he crossed the threshold. Kern followed on Miltiades's heels, Jacob and Trandon behind him.

Noph hesitated, looking back down the corridor
the way they had come. No one else was present.
The two guards bore no weapons other than their
poleaxes, which were too elaborately decorated to
be true battlefield weapons. Noph thought he
smelled some sort of liquor, like rum, in the air. The
red-faced guards stared at each other, ignoring the
youth. They seemed to have the same skin rash
that others in the palace had—nasty stuff. The
flesh of one man's cheek seemed dry, flaky, almost . . . scaly. Noph glanced at Garkim, who indi-
cated with a gesture that he should enter the room.

Noph turned and went into the chamber after
the others, but he stayed close to the door, thinking Garkim might shut them all in. Nothing of the
sort happened. Garkim casually followed him into
the illuminated hall, pulling the great door shut
as he did and giving the youth an empty smile.

"There is no mage-king here," called Miltiades,
his voice echoing in the vastness of the room. He
had undone the thong on his warhammer, and the
weapon dangled from his right hand, ready for
use. "You are a liar, Garkim."

Noph stopped and stared around the great
room in astonishment. This was a throne room? It
was huge, but there was no furniture, and the
room had a dank odor to it. The walls, as high as
three-story buildings, were covered with floor-
length red curtains. The ceiling was a great length
of high rafters from which a few globes cast a dim,
watery magical light over all.

"I did not lie," said Garkim mildly, walking past
the stunned Noph. "The mage-king is here." He
approached the other four men, who warily took

up positions in a semicircle facing him.

"Noph, open the door!" ordered Kern, pointing with his free hand. Startled, the youth backed up and reached for the door handle there.

"We are here," said a deep voice that filled the chamber.

The men in the room—all but Garkim—whirled, searching for the source.

"Then show yourself!" Miltiades called out angrily. "We have come too far and lost too much already to be amused by trickery!"

"There is no trickery here," said the voice. "This is where we meet our guests. We are the emperor of Doegan." There was no anger in the voice. There was no feeling in it at all.

Garkim waited patiently, standing with hands clasped before him, while the four men before him continued looking around the room. Their weapons were readied but at the moment useless as toothpicks.

"You are here to find Lady Eidola of Neverwinter, the intended bride of the Open Lord of Waterdeep, Piergeiron Paladinson," continued the voice. "The High Mage of Waterdeep, Khelben Arunsun, who is called the Blackstaff, determined that this city of Eldrinpar was where Lady Eidola's kidnappers had taken her. You are here to find Lady Eidola and to destroy the thing that prevents Khelben Arunsun from magically scrying our city, so that he may determine where Lady Eidola is being held and send such assistance as you may need to rescue her and bring her back to Waterdeep."

None of the men answered. Kern, Trandon, Jacob, and Noph stared at Miltiades, who turned to stare at Lord Garkim. Garkim returned the stare impassively.

"Miltiades of Phlan," said the voice.

"Yes," said the paladin, his tone dangerously low.

"Lord Garkim has spoken to you of the blood-forges."

Miltiades looked away from Garkim at the red-curtained walls around the room. "He has. Why do you not show yourself?"

"We are here. We meet with you as is our custom."

"Is it because of your bloodforge?" Miltiades scanned the room at eye level, then squinted up at the rafters. "Do you not appear before us person-ally because you wish to conceal some power of your bloodforge?"

"We are here before you, Miltiades of Phlan. We are very near you in body. We meet with you in this manner because there is no other way to meet with you."

"You're with us more in spirit than body, maybe?" said Jacob. Miltiades and the others looked at him. He gave a wry smile and shrugged. "Couldn't think of anything else to say," he said apologetically.

"I don't get this," said Kern. He moved away from the others toward the long wall to the right of the door they had entered. "This is the craziest meeting with a king I have ever had."

"Miltiades of Phlan."

"Speak your mind," said the paladin sharply, starting to walk toward the wall on the left side of the room from the door. Jacob caught on and began walking toward the far wall opposite the double doors, examining the curtains.

"Lord Garkim explained the nature and powers of the bloodforges to you."

"He did not explain very much," said the paladin. He reached the wall and carefully began to probe the thick red curtains with the head of his warhammer. They seemed normal enough. He pushed in, and the hammer head thumped into the wall behind.

He abruptly looked down at his left hand. The ring given to him by his wife Evaine was glowing faintly. Poison? Where?

"A bloodforge was used to kidnap Lady Eidola," said the voice. "It was not the bloodforge of Doegan that was involved in this act. Your lady was taken by the bloodforge of Ysdar."

Miltiades snorted skeptically. He carefully knelt down by the curtain, so that the wall was on his left side. With his left hand, he reached down and picked up the bottom of the curtain. He raised his hammer with his right hand and prepared to strike, expecting a venomous creature.

Behind the curtain was a solid black wall, its surface slick and glossy. Miltiades smelled mildew and must, noting cobwebs were pulled away as he lifted the curtain's bottom. He looked back at Lord Garkim, who watched him intently without moving, arms folded in front of him.

"Who is Ysdar?" said Kern, far across the room. He poked the curtain before him. A low clunk sounded through the room.

"Ysdar is the leader of the Fallen Temple, an evil cult within our lands. We are not sure of Ysdar's present or former identity. The cult preys upon all peoples in all countries here. It has captured or excavated its own bloodforge and now uses it against our imperial domain and all other kingdoms and states in this region. Ysdar is the spirit of annihilation. Were you to destroy the bloodforge that shields our domain from Ysdar's legions, you would doom us and all our subjects. The Imperial Reaches of Doegan would be an eroded wasteland in less than a decade."

Noph spoke up, gazing up at the ceiling. "What is the Fallen Temple? We hardly know a thing about it, no disrespect to Lord Garkim here."

"The Fallen Temple is the twisted remnant of the most powerful of the five Temples of the Southern Clave which joined the Right Armada, the fleet assembled and led by our ancestor, King Aetheric I, from the Moonshae Islands to the shores of our Utter East. As divine punishment for the vile offenses committed by the priests of this temple during the voyage of the Right Armada to the Utter East, all priests of this temple were stripped of their holy powers and spells. As mundane punishment for endangering their fellow voyagers, they were stripped of their right to vote at the last Great Council, and they gained no collective or individual fiefs from the Founding Lords as they divided up the Utter East.

"These heretics, bitter at their punishment, sought out other high powers that would invest them with a semblance of their former abilities. Their descendants found a patron native to this land, a corrupt and ancient entity that has sought to destroy all life here, from ourself down to the lowest beggar. The bloodforge of Doegan is our shield against this wickedness. Your plan to destroy our shield would reduce all you see to ruin. You would murder our empire for the life of one woman."

"Miltiades," called Kern. Everyone turned to look. The youthful warrior in the golden armor was holding up the bottom of the red curtain nearest him. Behind it was a wall of mortared stone.

"There's a rock wall back here, too," called Jacob.

Miltiades looked up. He tugged the curtain bottom, then stood and jerked. The top of the curtain tore free of several spikes holding it up near the ceiling. Miltiades hauled back on the curtain abruptly. It ripped and fell away in the center, tearing further as he walked backward, still gripping the cloth.

Behind the curtain on the left wall was a vast jet wall, shiny though smudged with dust. The wall seemed to have depth to it, looking less like polished marble than like dark, almost opaque glass. Miltiades dropped the curtain. The whole center of the wall was now revealed in the steady light from the ceiling globes.

Lord Garkim cleared his throat. "That was not polite, nor was it wise," he said to Miltiades, in mild irritation.

Miltiades did not answer. He stared intently at the black wall. Far above him, the globes of light nearest the wall dimmed. The shadows of the paladins lengthened and stretched before them to the shining wall.

Jacob and Kern quickly headed toward Miltiades. Trandon carefully reached up and put his right hand inside his vest again, his left hand clutching his tall quarterstaff. Noph thought about pulling out one of his knives. Something was very strange about this place. He turned, saw that he was near the door out of the room, and moved over to it. He reached for the door handle again, making sure it would open.

As he did, the door gave a low thump, as if something had been moved against it. He seized the door handle and shoved on it hard. It did not move. He threw his shoulder against it, accomplishing nothing. "Locked!" he shouted, a shred of terror flooding into his voice. "We're locked in!"

"Garkim!" Miltiades shouted, tearing his gaze from the wall and spinning on his heel. He lunged for the councilor and seized him by the front of his ship-decorated tabard. "Garkim, what thing is hidden behind that wall?" he roared in the smaller man's face.

Garkim glared up at the larger man. His dark eyes were bright with rage. "You will know very soon," he said quietly. "You are not a wise man, and your manners are barbaric. You are hardly better than your ancestral brothers were when they lost their holy powers and turned their grand church into the Fallen Temple."

"What are you talking about?" the big warrior growled.

Garkim measured his next words. "I am talking about the Fallen Temple. In these lands it is also known as the Temple of the Broken Hammer."

Miltiades suddenly froze. The rage melted from his face. His mouth fell open as his eyes grew wide.

"Tyr's church?" Miltiades whispered. He sounded like a child. "That was *Tyr's* church?"

Only Garkim's burning eyes answered him.

The warrior's hand relaxed, releasing Garkim's

clothing. Miltiades took a step back, his face
drained of color. "Great Tyr above," he gasped. His
right hand fell open, letting his warhammer
dangle from the strap on his wrist. "Great Righteous Tyr, that couldn't have happened. You lied to
Kern when you said—"

"I knew you would not welcome the news," said
Garkim with disdain. "I was unsure of your reaction and wished to err on the side of caution. After
all, your holy church of Tyr brought evil into our
land. I did not know if you would do the same."

"Lord Garkim speaks the truth," said the room-
filling voice. No one turned to look for it. "Patriarch Justarvis, High Avenger of Tyr's Church of
the Southern Clave of the Moonshaes, fell in with
the priests of Tempus, the depraved Count Boarswic, and the rapacious Northmen. Justarvis was
convinced to take vengeance on every ship and
town that would not offer their plague-stricken
ships refuge and healing. The patriarch and his
followers looted and burned and murdered, calling
their acts righteous and deserved punishments for
their victims. For his many foul deeds, the patriarch was rewarded by your god Tyr with a hideous
death, caught in the arms of a kraken and dragged
screaming with his bodyguards into the depths of
the Great Sea, mere hours before our shores were
sighted and the Right Armada landed."

"That's a lie!" screamed Jacob, wild-eyed, looking at the black wall. His grip on his huge two-
handed blade tightened. "The gods damn your
lying tongue!"

There was silence for the space of three heart-
beats.

"That was no lie," said the voice. "And we are damned already."

A low rumbling rolled through the room, coming from the shiny black wall. It sounded less like an earthquake than the stirring of a great amount of water.

Miltiades whirled, facing the wall. His face held a strange look upon it. "Get away from that wall!" he roared. Everyone but Garkim backed up a dozen steps, their eyes locked on the blackness.

"What's happening?" asked Noph, his voice shaking. He was trying to get the hunting knife from his boot, but couldn't make his fingers stop trembling long enough to untie the straps.

Kern made the sign of the hammer over his face and chest with his left hand. The rumbling was louder, resounded now like thunder within the chamber. "Could it be an earthquake?" he called to Miltiades. "Tyr save us, what's going on?" He stopped backing away and hefted his hammer uncertainly, as if readying to cast it at the wall.

"Lower your weapons!" Garkim shouted at Kern, uncrossing his arms. Desperation filled his words. "You will kill everyone if you attack! The wall is all that separates us from the emperor! Lower your weapons! You cannot attack him without killing us all!"

The lights dimmed further, and the surface of the wall appeared to grow more transparent. Something moved within it. A thick, snakelike shape with yellow scales as large as plates rolled into view, pressed briefly against the opposite side of the wall, then pulled back into the darkness. It was as wide across as a man is tall.

Everyone but Garkim fell back several paces.

"It's a water tank!" shouted Trandon. Shock and horror radiated from his features. "The wall is glass! Don't break it, or we'll drown here!"

"Tyr guide me and give me strength," whispered Miltiades through bloodless lips. He swallowed as his eyes drank in the ghastly sight.

Another snakelike tentacle, coiling in the black water beyond, appeared and pressed itself to the wall. This time the tentacle remained, its scaly skin covered with cancerous wounds. Peeling, rotting skin trailed in the water around it. Noph felt a terrible urge to flee as another tentacle appeared to the right and pressed against the glasslike wall.

A hand with fingers as big around as tree limbs appeared out of the darkness. The fingertips brushed the glass with a rough thump, then retreated and vanished. Another great stirring of water rumbled through the walls and floor.

A vast, faint object, oval in shape, appeared beyond the wall. It drifted forward until everyone in the room could see it clearly.

Jacob nearly dropped his great sword. He staggered back, his eyes the size of moons. Kern and Miltiades froze open-mouthed, warhammers raised and arm muscles tight. Trandon shielded his eyes and crouched down, his quarterstaff rolling away on the floor.

Noph choked on his terror. He could not look away from the beautiful, inhuman face that almost touched the far side of the wall.

"We are here," said the voice in the room. "We are the emperor of Doegan."

Chapter 7

Promises to Keep

"You are a monster," said Miltiades, breaking the awful silence.

"We are the emperor," said the voice in the air. The thin lips of the yellow-gray monstrosity on the other side of the wall did not move. Enormous round eyes, black as shiny onyx and as large as windows, stared out at the group. The nose was broad, the nostrils each an arm span across. A pattern of scales ran over the face but did not mar its strange, ghastly beauty.

The reptilian coils at the bottom of the black wall twisted slowly around, ever in motion.

"Lord Garkim informed you that the blood-forges made certain alterations in those who used them," said the voice. "It is said that all kings of Doegan are fond of the sea. Our spiritual kinship with the sea, beginning even before the building of the Right Armada, has gradually taken on physical form. We can speak with the use of magic from our bloodforge, but such time is limited by the nature of the device. We will not be able to communicate with you much longer this day. We must take pains to be concise."

"We will not deal with evil!" shouted Noph, swiftly gathering heart. "We sense your true nature, and we reject you!"

"Noph!" roared Miltiades in warning.

"You know nothing of my true nature," said the voice. "I am not evil, as you know it."

Noph glanced at Miltiades, who looked back but did not confirm or deny the emperor's last statement. "He's lying, isn't he?" Noph shouted, pointing. "You said he was a monster! Look what the bloodforge did to him! How do we know he isn't going to kill or eat us?"

Miltiades swallowed but managed a grim smile before looking back at the awful, beautiful face. "We do not," he said. "Please forgive the young man. He is foolish and inexperienced." Noph slumped angrily and half-turned away.

"Let's talk about the Lady Eidola!" called Kern. "Tell us where she is right now, or I'll plant this hammer in your forehead and find her myself!"

"The water in our dwelling is poisonous, Kern of Phlan. It is excreted by our skin, and it is hostile to all living things. Should the wall between us be broken, you would swim in liquid death. It would eat the flesh from your bones while you screamed and choked. Your own wife would not recognize your remains."

Silence fell again for a few moments.

"Tell me where Lady Eidola is," Miltiades repeated, only slightly subdued.

"She has been captured by the forces of Ysdar of the Fallen Temple," said the voice. "We believe she is being held somewhere here in our own city, but is so warded that not even we can detect her location. You are right in your belief that the power that prevents outsiders from spying upon us with magic is generated by our bloodforge. It is an invisible shield woven by ourself. We will not take it down. Fiends and bloodforge armies would fight over the rubble of our empire within a decade were we to lower our defenses. There are more crucial issues for our city and our land than your quest for a petty noble's fiancee. You will hear us out on this matter, then make your choice."

Kern, Jacob, Trandon, and Noph looked at Miltiades for his reaction.

"Speak," the warrior growled, forcing the word out. "We will hear you out, but we promise you no more than that."

"The bloodforge generates an enormous degree of magical potential, which can be harvested by its user and converted into actual magical ability. We were not born a wizard, Miltiades of Phlan. We

were born a normal man, destined to rule like our
father, who was also a normal man, though the
bloodforge had already altered him so that he was
forced to spend the better part of each day bathing
in a tub to keep his skin moist. We were changed
more than he, because we learned early in life how
to unlock the full potential of the bloodforge, and so
took on more of its alterations than our ancestors."

"You took on its curse," corrected Miltiades.

"Our body is not our bloodforge's true curse,
Miltiades of Phlan. Our bloodforge gathers its
magical potential from the land around it. This
ancient land is soaked in magical power. Our
bloodforge drains the magic in the earth, buried
under the soil, rock, and water, and offers it for
our use. But as the magic drains from the land, it
drains too from a great barrier-ward that was
placed upon this region ages ago, by the ancestors
of the Mar. The barrier-ward has weakened from
long use of the bloodforges by all the reigning
lords and kings, and it barely separates our world
from that which it was meant to seal off. The curse
of the bloodforges, Miltiades of Phlan, is that they
have left us vulnerable to outworld horrors who
would feed upon us as hungry magpies feed on
worms. Their use has nearly bred our ruin."

Kern blinked. The reflections of himself and his
allies in the polished black wall had for a moment
seemed to blend with the great tentacles of the
monster-emperor visible on the wall's other side.
He thought he had seen himself and his party
caught in those slowly twisting coils.

"I cannot imagine any outworld horror worse
than yourself," Kern muttered darkly.

"Then you have a very poor imagination, Kern of Phlan. Lord Garkim will show you documents and bring you sages that confirm the truth of our words. Two months ago, we took pains to ward our city against attacks by tanar'ri from the Abyss, which were given knowledge of our blood-forge by Ysdar's agents. As we now speak, our city is slowly becoming besieged by fiends and monsters that lurk in the savanna and jungle around us, looking for a way past our walls to wrap their clawed fingers around our bloodforge and carry it away. The human debris that bows to Ysdar creeps past our gates, and the Fallen Temple grows stronger in our realm with each sunset. Our doom is truly at hand."

"Tanar'ri," said Trandon, getting to his feet. Though pale, he had gained control of himself again. "We fought tanar'ri, big vulturelike vrocks, at the gate in Undermountain that brought us here."

"They were doubtless among the first of the army that is arrayed against us, an army that is strengthening by the hour. There is but one course left to us all. You cannot destroy our bloodforge merely to allow Khelben Arunsun to see you through his crystal ball. Your gate to Undermountain is destroyed, and you are trapped within these walls with the rest of us. Our enemy is your own. You must work with us against our mutual foe."

"We did not come here to fight your wars," said Miltiades in abrupt dismissal. "We came to find Lady Eidola and open the way for her to go home, and no more."

The gigantic face in the black wall shifted,

turning slightly to look directly down at the silver-armored warrior with its empty black eyes.

"We feel no pity for you, Miltiades of Phlan," said the voice. "You choose your own path in life and proudly bear the consequences. But we feel great sorrow for Lady Eidola, who is now in the hands of Ysdar's agents. She is no doubt becoming very familiar with the peculiar ways of Ysdar, the secret lord of the Fallen Temple, that creation of Tyr's justice-loving priests who contaminated our empire with their holy filth two and a quarter centuries ago. Is it not ironic that the righteousness of Tyr's paladins now throws her forever into the claws of cannibals and torturers who were themselves once among Tyr's chosen?"

"Liar!" roared Kern. His hammer arm whipped over and down.

"No!" shouted Miltiades. Garkim uttered a strangled cry, leaping forward as if he thought he could fly through space and seize Kern's hammer as it spun through the air at the mage-king's impassive face.

The hammer slammed into the wall directly between the mage-king's eyes. It rebounded with an ear-splitting crash, flying back to smash into the stone floor behind the crouching Trandon. Dust filled the air. Stone chips rang from metal armor.

Breathless, everyone stared at the hammer, then at the black wall. There was no mark on it.

The gigantic beautiful face had not once changed expression.

"Lord Garkim," said the voice. "You must forgive us for not mentioning to you long ago that this wall, though transparent like glass, is impervious to all physical forces. You would then have been able to warn our guests of this and thus prevent embarrassing mishaps."

Garkim stared at the hammer on the floor, too stunned to speak.

"My time grows short," the voice said. "Miltiades of Phlan, we challenge you to ask your god if you and your comrades should join forces with such as us. Our wards do not prevent communication with divine powers. The fate of our empire and your lady, if not the city of Waterdeep as well, hangs by a thread this day. Pray to your mighty Tyr and see if you will sever that thread or save it."

Miltiades glared hard at the empty black orbs. He was a fool to even think about this. The choices were so obvious. The mage-king was not to be trusted. Miltiades should lead his force out of this trap and set about escaping from the palace, then use the necklace to locate Lady Eidola. Nothing was simpler.

And yet . . .

Distrusting the mage-king, Miltiades cleared his mind and closed his eyes.

His comrades nervously watched as he did, glancing back and forth from him to the mage-king's face. A half-minute passed.

Miltiades opened his eyes. He lowered his weapon, seeming to relax. Then he stood stiffly straight and began tying his hammer to his belt by its strap.

Kern's mouth fell open in astonishment. Trandon, Jacob, and Noph looked at one another in confusion. Lord Garkim frowned, clearly surprised.

When Miltiades finished, he looked up at the beautiful face.

"We will destroy the enemies of Doegan," he said to the face, "and we will find Lady Eidola. On this you have my word." Then he turned and walked toward the doors. The doors thumped as he reached them. The paladin put his hand on a handle and pulled one of the two doors open with ease. He looked back at the others. "Well, come along," he said, as if speaking to children.

Kern retrieved his hammer. He and the others silently followed the paladin out, leaving only Lord Garkim behind. Miltiades looked back at Lord Garkim before he left with a curiously calm expression, then shut the door.

Lord Garkim looked back at the great black eyes floating above him. "Your Majesty, what did . . . ah, did you do something to—"

"We did nothing to him. He prayed to his deity. He will join us in our fight against Ysdar. We calculated a high probability that he would be told to do so by Tyr."

Garkim shook his head in wonder. "Your Majesty, he is a holy warrior, an instrument of his deity. I could not see how he could be ordered to take up our cause. He regards us as enemies, and—"

"You are correct, Lord Garkim," said the voice. The face began to withdraw from the black wall, fading into the darkness and pulling its coils back with it. The room rumbled as water shifted and sloshed in the distance. "You are correct. We *are* his enemies. We believe Tyr told him to liberate this land from our rule, from the tyranny of the bloodforges. He did not truly take up our cause. He said, 'We will destroy the enemies of Doegan,' by which he meant us, Lord Garkim—we, your emperor, as well as Ysdar, the Fallen Temple, the tanar'ri, and all beasts that inhabit this Utter East who dare oppose him. He left because he could do nothing else here; he will not waste his time on futile gestures. He is very wise, this Miltiades of Phlan. You must be prepared to kill him soon, Lord Garkim."

The last words had not fully settled into Lord Garkim's mind by the time the mage-king had fully vanished into the depths of blackness beyond the great wall. When they did, Garkim caught his breath, staggered at the implications. Kill Miltiades? This was a dangerous task indeed, the hardest he had ever been given. It was not a challenge he welcomed. It would have to be done, certainly, but how? He would have to kill or disable the other visitors, too, but they would be less of a problem. Poison was out, thanks to that ring Miltiades wore, and that other paladin was immune to most magical effects. This would be a serious problem.

And there was the curious thing that happened after Miltiades had prayed. Suddenly, Lord Garkim could no longer read the silver warrior's mind. Instead of the usual stream of thoughts, Garkim could pick up only a chanted prayer to Tyr from the paladin's thoughts. It reminded him uncomfortably of his parents' old trick. This was a bad development. Why had the paladin started this? Did he suspect . . . ?

Lord Garkim looked after the vanished mageking, then slowly walked to the chamber exit.

"Lord Garkim," said the voice in the air.

"Yes, Your Majesty," he replied, never breaking stride.

"Send triple our usual offering to the Temple of Umberlee this evening. Then speak with Wavelord Gethonar if you feel the need for additional advice or assistance in this matter."

Garkim stopped for a moment, then resumed his walk. "Why, thank you, Your Majesty," he said as he left. There was no reply.

The story continues . . .

The DOUBLE DIAMOND TRIANGLE SAGA™

The bride of the Open Lord of Waterdeep has been abducted. The kidnappers are from the far-off lands of the Utter East. But who are they? And what do they really want? Now a group of brave paladins must travel to the perilous kingdoms of this unknown land to find the answers. But in this mysterious world, nothing is ever quite what it appears.

Look for the forthcoming books in the series

The Paladins
(January 1998)

The Mercenaries
(January 1998)

Errand of Mercy
(February 1998)

An Opportunity for Profit
(March 1998)

Conspiracy
(April 1998)

Uneasy Alliances
(May 1998)

Easy Betrayals
(June 1998)

The Diamond
(July 1998)

Coming in March

AN OPPORTUNITY FOR PROFIT
By Dave Gross

The pirates hired to assassinate the kidnapped Waterdeep bride are hot on the trail. Having landed on the shores of the Utter East, they face fiendish perils and desperate dangers—all without knowing the identity of their employer. Now fate has set them on a collision course with others whose motives are quite different from their own.

Coming in April

CONSPIRACY
By J. Robert King

As the search continues in the Utter East for the kidnapped bride of Waterdeep, the forces of the paladins and mercenaries converge. Now, for the first time, the dark secret behind the abduction is revealed, a mighty force is released from its bonds, and the searchers realize their quest is only half begun.

Coming in May

UNEASY ALLIANCES
By David Cook with Peter Archer

Paladins and mercenaries have joined forces to defeat an attacking army of fiends. Now a powerful new weapon, the bloodforge, comes into their hands. But some suspect that their leader's plans for the weapon are less than honorable. Can they undermine his hidden motives, while holding off the fiendish army?